A STORM AT

PEBBLE BEACH

HARRY FORSE

A STORM AT

PEBBLE BEACH

HARRY FORSE

Sleeping Bear Press

PUBLISHER

Sleeping Bear Press
310 North Main
P.O. Box 20
Chelsea, Michigan 48118
www.sleepingbearpress.com

Printed and bound in The United States.
10 9 8 7 6 5 4 3 2 1

Library of Congress Cataloging-in-Publication Data
Forse, Harry.
A Storm at Pebble Beach / by Harry Forse.
p. cm.
ISBN 1-886947-84-8
1. Pebble Beach Golf Links (Pebble Beach, Calif.)-Fiction.
2. Pebble Beach (Calif.)-Fiction. 3. Golfers-Fiction.

PS3556.O7398 S86 2000
813'.6-dc21   00-025953

I maintain that golf and tournament golf are two different things.

—Robert T. Jones, Jr.

The 18th hole is one of the best finishing holes I've ever played. The course impressed me so much that any time they have another tournament here, you can bank on my being here.

—Tour professional Al Watrous, 1926

CHAPTER 1

The day's final foursome was making its way up the 18th fairway in carts. Kevin Courtney waved at the golfers as he walked in the opposite direction. His evening pilgrimage at Pebble Beach Golf Links had become a ritual.

After busy hours of overseeing his staff, supervising the ordering and selling of merchandise, attending meetings, giving lessons, lunching and occasionally teeing it up with dignitaries, and making himself available to the media—normal duties of the head professional at the country's greatest public golf course—Kevin needed to unwind.

Today, as he did every day, he walked onto the 18th tee. He went to the back edge and looked down at the massive rocks rising out of the surf a dozen feet below. He inhaled deeply of the wind blowing sharply off Carmel Bay, so laden with water it was almost a mist. Often it was dark by the time he got here. Now, in the twilight, he could see the waves cresting and breaking onto the pebbled beach that gave the course its name. He could also hear the thunder of their crashing in a cadence as rhythmic as that of a metronome.

He lifted his head and felt the spray on his tanned face—just as he had done the first time he played Pebble 15 years before. A senior at Sacramento High School at the time, he had qualified to play in the state Amateur. That was the beginning of his love affair with Pebble Beach, an affection that grew each time he played the fabled course.

Six months previously, the pressure of five years on the PGA Tour forced him to look for a club position. At the same time—as luck would have it—Pebble Beach was searching for a "name golfer" to head up their operation. Kevin had won three times on tour, was once runner-up at the Masters, and was one of the game's better-known players. From his first day on the job, it had been a perfect match—so perfect, in fact, that only a month before, in January, he'd been given a new five-year contract through 1994.

A distant foghorn sounded as he again felt the salty spray on his face. God, how he loved this place. To be head pro here was a fantasy he never dreamed would come true. He looked out over Carmel Bay, then heard the ring of his cell phone.

"Glad I got you, Kev."

"What's up?" he asked his attorney, cupping a hand over his ear to block out the Pacific's roar.

"Judge Higgins has to go to a meeting in Washington next week. He moved the hearing up to this Thursday."

"That's the first day of the tournament."

"I know."

Kevin shook his head. The AT&T Pebble Beach National Pro-Am was the biggest event of the year. To be gone several hours in the middle of the day...

"You still there?"

"Yes, and I'll be here on Thursday, too," he told Brad Hilligoss. Kevin and Brad had been teammates on the golf team at Stanford; Brad stayed to get a degree in law, while Kevin—after an abortive few months in the business world —joined a minitour.

"This may change your mind," Hilligoss said. "Higgins's calendar is booked solid. It's Thursday or three months."

"Three months! That would be May."

"You golfers do know your math."

The eight hours Kevin had spent with his young son Joey the previous Saturday had seemed more like eight minutes. To wait two weeks for another eight hours, then another two weeks, and another... "How long will the hearing last?"

"Two or three hours, minimum."

Kevin looked in the direction of the town of Carmel, not much more than a mile away. He pictured a seven-year-old boy doing his homework, watching cartoons on television and eating an early dinner, no doubt with a babysitter. Kevin's ex-wife would be showing a home, going after a listing or attending some meeting. To Kevin's way of thinking, she didn't seem to spend that much time with Joey. In that regard, he was as good a father as she was a mother—better in a lot of ways.

"Higgins owed me a favor, Kev. I called it in on this one."

Kevin had been biting his lip so hard it hurt. He ran a hand through his blond hair. Joey's was almost the same color but not quite as bleached from the sun.

"Kevin?"

"Okay, all right. I don't see that I have much choice."

"Excellent. What are you doing tonight?"

"Having dinner with a friend here for the tournament."

"Well, look," Brad said. "Tomorrow I have to be in San

Francisco. I'll be there all day tomorrow and Wednesday. That means we need to get together tonight to prepare for the hearing."

"I thought we went over everything last week."

"Got a few more things I need to cover."

Kevin sighed. "I'll be there in an hour."

"It won't take long," Brad said. "You should still be able to keep your dinner engagement."

Kevin switched off the phone and started back to the pro shop. He tried to recapture the tranquillity he had felt a few minutes earlier, but the salty breeze blowing off Carmel Bay and across Pebble's 18th fairway was no match for the upcoming custody battle over his son.

Kevin and Joan had dated during their junior and senior years in college and had gotten married after graduation. She obtained a real estate license; he went to work in a brokerage office and spent the longest six months of his life trying to peddle stocks and bonds before quitting to join a California golf tour.

That was the beginning of the end of the marriage. Joan thought Kevin was lazy and immature. He often felt that she was more interested in her career than in him. Her surprise pregnancy and Joey's birth prolonged the marriage two more years. By that time Kevin was playing golf all over the country. Lonely and unhappy, he had his first and only one-night stand and got caught. Joan immediately filed for divorce. He didn't contest it, but did contest her attempt to gain full custody of their son.

It was granted, though, largely on the grounds that Kevin was gone most of the time, and he was only allowed to have Joey one day every other week. It wasn't so bad when he was on the road. Now that he was here all the time, though, and Joey was so close...it seemed to Kevin that it would be easier if he were a thousand miles away.

Hope mixed with anxiety as he parked in front of a narrow, one-story structure near downtown Carmel, where the actor Clint Eastwood had once been mayor. Many buildings were narrow in the artsy-touristy town that didn't have stoplights or streetlights or neon signs or tall buildings. Carmel land was precious. Brad's firm had paid more than a million for their small piece of property.

Kevin's gold Seiko showed 6:35 as he strode up a brick sidewalk to a massive oak door. Above it was an arched recess, beside it a brass plate: Brady, Hilligoss & Jones. The large brass doorknob turned with difficulty and he stepped into the long, narrow foyer lighted by a tall lamp on a Chippendale table.

Brad Hilligoss's office was straight ahead, the door open, but to darkness. There wasn't the usual aroma of cigar smoke drifting out into the foyer, either. Kevin smelled only furniture polish as he walked to the open door and looked inside. No Brad. Someone had to be here or the front door wouldn't be unlocked. He switched on the light, but was too antsy to sit in one of the brown leather chairs.

Suddenly the hollow, staccato sound of high heels echoed from the foyer's hardwood floor. Kevin spun around to see a woman approaching.

"Mr. Courtney?" she said, extending her hand. "I'm Sara Arnold, an attorney with the firm."

She was wearing a black business suit, with a white blouse buttoned high at the neck. Kevin judged her to be younger than his thirty-two years and at least eight inches shorter than his six feet. He took the offered hand, felt and returned a strong grip, and released it.

"I'm sorry to have to tell you this," she said. "But Mr. Hilligoss experienced chest pains shortly after he talked to you. He had to be taken to the hospital."

"My God!"

"Mr. Brady is with him. He just called and said they are running a series of tests."

"They don't know anything?"

"Not yet. Before he would leave, though, Mr. Hilligoss gave me your file and insisted on briefing me on the background of your case. I've only had a few minutes to review the material. Shall we go into my office?"

"Wait; you'll be handling it?"

"Let's hope Mr. Hilligoss can. Mr. Brady and Mr. Jones both have commitments for Thursday morning, which preclude their becoming involved. Therefore, it's possible that you might get stuck with me."

"I didn't..." Kevin's voice trailed off.

"If it would make you feel more secure, Mr. Courtney," Sara said with a wry smile, "I can get one of Mr. Hilligoss's cigars and light up."

Grinning sheepishly, Kevin shook his head.

"I'm in the front." She turned away and Kevin followed her into an office half the size of Brad's. Still, there was room for a large mahogany desk with a swivel chair, two brown leather chairs, and a small round table. Kevin noticed a gray folder on the table as Brad's replacement turned to face him, hands on her hips.

"I fight as hard as any man, Mr. Courtney. No, I'm not as experienced as Mr. Hilligoss. But I was a Rhodes scholar, I graduated number one in my class, and I know the law." She paused. "The choice is yours. We can spend more time trying to sell you on Sara Arnold, or we can roll up our sleeves and get to work."

"Work," Kevin said.

"I thought we'd be more comfortable at the table." Sara pulled up a chair, and Kevin sat across from her. She had short black hair, little makeup, and dark eyes.

"You're seeking joint custody."

"Yes."

"Mr. Hilligoss explained to you the three conditions that have to be met for the court to modify a custody order?"

Kevin nodded. "The circumstances have to change, it has to be beneficial to Joey, and the present arrangement has to be harmful to him. 'Injurious,' I believe Brad called it."

"That third condition may be our biggest obstacle."

"What's *injurious* is for Joey to only be with his father one day every two weeks."

"That's what we have to prove to the judge." She opened the folder. "I understand that you were off playing golf professionally when the original custody order was issued."

"You make it sound like I was some kind of a playboy. I was competing on a professional tour, working my tail off playing or practicing seven days a week."

"Now you're the head pro at Pebble Beach."

"That's right. I'm home as much or more than Joan. She's always out working on her real estate business."

Again Sara checked the folder. "You live at 2617 Devon. Where is that?"

"A condo in east Carmel, only seven blocks from Joey's school."

"Does anyone live with you?"

"No."

"And you aren't on any tour, doing a lot of traveling?"

"No."

"Who would take care of Joey when he's not in school and you're at work?"

"That's all been arranged with a retired teacher who lives in my complex."

"You work weekends?"

"Occasionally. Not very often."

"I thought Saturday and Sunday were the busiest days on a golf course."

"Every day's busy at Pebble Beach."

The questions and answers—as many about Joan and her lifestyle as about Kevin—continued and Sara filled several sheets of paper with notes. It was nearly an hour later when she put them in the gray folder and closed it.

"I think we're ready for Thursday, Kevin—if I may call you that."

"Of course."

"Any questions?"

"What are my chances, Sara?"

"What did Mr. Hilligoss tell you?"

"'Pretty good, but don't count on it.'"

"I don't know that I can improve on that. Let's hope he can make it. If not, I'll fight for you and Joey as if he were my own son. Any other questions?"

Kevin shook his head.

"Okay. Please be here at 9:30 Thursday morning."

"Isn't the hearing at 10:00?"

"Yes."

"I'll be at the courthouse at 10:00. I need to spend every possible minute at the course."

Her eyes hardened. "Are 30 minutes that important?"

No, they weren't. "Okay, Sara, 9:30...here."

The clock showed 7:48 when Kevin headed the black Riviera back to Pebble Beach. He found himself wondering if Brad would recover quickly enough to take back the case; he seemed wimpy compared to Sara Arnold. It was a selfish thought, one he relegated to a back recess of his mind.

There were so many other things to think about, especially the pro shop—making sure there was enough merchandise, and that it was displayed properly for the thousands of souvenir-hunting spectators who would overrun the place. He had a breakfast meeting the next day, then would go nonstop for 12 to 14 hours. But it was work he loved; he belonged on a golf course. *This course*, he thought for the thousandth time as he turned off 17-Mile Drive and drove toward the pro shop. *His* pro shop.

Kevin was planning to meet Ken Fuller in the Terrace Lounge. He entered The Lodge, described in the *Course Guide to Pebble Beach Golf Links* as "an enclave of tradition, elegance and gracious hospitality," and started for the Terrace when someone tapped him on the shoulder. It was Laura Appleby, hostess at the Cypress Room, the grandest of the four restaurants in The Lodge. Four months earlier, he had helped her son—who was speech and hearing impaired—get a job on the maintenance crew at the course. She couldn't have been more grateful.

"I need to talk to you," she said, surprising Kevin by taking his hand and leading him toward an empty coatroom. She was wearing a red knit dress and, as always, her shoulder-length black hair was perfectly styled. The only thing missing was her smile.

Laura closed the door behind them. "I only have a minute,

Kevin. You know I lip-read, right, because of my son?"

He nodded.

"Well earlier this evening, Mr. Leonard was having dinner with Mr. Komoto. At one point, he said..." Laura put a hand on her chest and took a deep breath. "He pointed toward the golf course and said, '*Mansions* will soon be rising out there.'"

Confused, Kevin stared at her. "*Who* said this?"

"Mr. Komoto." Masaru Komoto was the Japanese owner of Pebble Beach.

"Mansions?"

"That's what he said."

"You're positive?"

"Yes."

Mansions, Kevin mouthed. *Mansions*. "Could he have been saying *thousands*? Maybe he was talking about all the spectators that will be here this week."

She shook her head vigorously. "He was facing directly toward me. I'm positive he said 'mansions will be rising out there.'"

Kevin had grasped at a straw, hoping it wasn't what Komoto had said. But a rapidly growing knot in the pit of his stomach told him that Laura Appleby hadn't misread the lips of the man who controlled the destiny of Pebble Beach.

"They can't do that, can they, Kevin?" she asked, squeezing his arm. "I'd lose my job." Blinking rapidly, she added, "So would Ryan."

"How long ago was this?"

"They just left. I think they were going to Mr. Leonard's house for an after-dinner drink."

"Laura, did you tell anyone else about this?"

"No."

"Good," Kevin said. "Please don't. Let me check it out first."
He patted her shoulder. "Don't worry. Maybe they were talking about something else, and it isn't as grim as it sounds."

He went into the Terrace Lounge to beg off dinner with Ken
Fuller, or at least tell him there would be a lengthy delay. He
was searching for Ken when the bartender motioned him over.

"A Mr. Fuller called, Kevin. He said there was a serious ill-
ness in his family and he couldn't make it tonight. He also
said he wouldn't be playing in the tournament."

"Goodness," Kevin replied, "it *must* be serious. Thanks,
Bill." Kevin felt sympathy for his friend, and he heard the
part about the tournament, but his mind had already returned
to Masaru Komoto. For years rumors of Pebble Beach's
demise had floated around, especially after the property was
purchased by the Japanese tycoon. He loved to gamble, and
some said the course was merely a stepping-stone to Las
Vegas. But that he would turn it into a real estate development was...unthinkable.

Jack Leonard, Kevin's boss, was the Director of Golf at
Pebble Beach. He lived near the course in a house that was
worth around $650,000—the lower end of the scale in a
neighborhood where ocean- or golf-front estates went for
several million. As luxurious as Jack's home was, rumor had
it that he was envious of those with a view of one or both of
the two P's: Pebble Beach and the Pacific.

Jo Leonard answered Kevin's ringing of the doorbell.

"Sorry to barge in on you like this, Jo, but I need to see Jack."

"I'm afraid he's having a meeting with Mr. Komoto, Kevin."

"Yes, I know."

Her eyebrows went up. "Uh, well, please wait here." She
was back in less than a minute. "I'm sorry, Kevin, but Jack said

they can't be disturbed. He said he could call you later tonight or he'll see you first thing in the morning. I'm sorry." She smiled.

"I'm sorry, too," Kevin said, and without hesitation he walked past her and down the hall he knew led to the den. Komoto and Leonard were sitting in tan leather captain's chairs, holding brandy snifters containing an amber-colored drink.

Leonard jumped to his feet. "What the hell?" he cried in the high-pitched voice that was so incongruous to his foot-ball-lineman build. "I told Jo we weren't to be disturbed."

Komoto appeared puzzled momentarily, but then his thin lips formed a mirthless smile. He nodded. Kevin returned the greeting. They had met in the pro shop five months before, the only time Kevin had seen the mysterious Japanese up close. He was nearly seventy but looked much younger. The five-foot-seven-inch business giant was wearing a black pinstripe suit, white shirt, and black and red tie.

"Dammit, Kevin," Leonard hissed, "what...?"

Komoto interrupted him. "Please join us, Mr. Courtney. The French outdid themselves with this delicious Grand Marnier, wouldn't you agree?"

"Mr. Komoto, are you selling Pebble Beach to a real estate developer?"

Leonard gasped. Komoto's eyes flashed for a moment, then he smiled. "Why do you ask such a question, Mr. Courtney?"

"Just wondering if it's true. Is it?"

"You're way out of line here, Kevin," Leonard said angrily. "There's no..."

Komoto put up a hand to silence him. "Where would you hear such a thing?"

"I'm around people all day, Mr. Komoto. I hear stuff."

"Ah, yes, the head professional of Pebble Beach." Komoto

took a sip of the liqueur without taking his eyes off Kevin, who was towering above him. He then patted his lips with the perfectly folded handkerchief from his breast pocket before carefully replacing it. "If I tell you what you wish to know, Mr. Courtney, may I have your word that it will not leave this room?"

Kevin nodded. There was something going on. His mind raced and his muscles tensed as he waited for the owner to continue.

"I am trying to play a charade, when obviously you already know the answer," Komoto said. "Yes, I am going to sell Pebble Beach to a real estate syndicate. Lots will be sold and the Pebble Beach Golf Links will soon only exist as a beautiful memory."

Kevin shook his head. "You *can't* be serious."

"I'm afraid so."

"You dumb son-of-a-bitch, Pebble Beach isn't just another golf course. It's like your Mount Fuji; it's a shrine, for God's sake. You *can't* destroy it."

"Oh, but I can, Mr. Courtney," Komoto said. "Your country is overrun with golf courses. In my country, only a fortunate few are privileged to actually play the game. For most, hitting balls at a practice facility is the closest they will ever get. Your country builds hundreds of new courses each year. Even a famous one such as this will not be missed."

"That's bullshit," Kevin said. "If you destroy Pebble Beach, you will be destroying part of the *soul* of golf. If you were a golfer, if you understood even the slightest thing about the game, you'd know that."

The owner shrugged his small shoulders. A rice farmer's son, he had turned out to be a genius at chemistry. At the age of twenty-four, Masaru developed a chemical that increased the efficiency of the fertilizer used in rice fields by 15 percent. He sold the formula to an agricultural giant for 15 million dollars, then shrewdly bought and sold businesses over the next 30 years. In time, he became one of the wealthiest men in Japan.

It was said that when Komoto bought Pebble Beach, he claimed never to have played golf. To Kevin's knowledge, he still hadn't.

Kevin looked at Leonard. "Jack, you can't let this happen."

His boss was still angry about the intrusion. "I have expressed to Mr. Komoto the same sentiments as *yours* many, many times. I'm afraid his mind is made up, and there is nothing that you or I can do about it."

Komoto took another sip from his snifter, then looked up at Kevin. "Now a question for you, Mr. Courtney. Have you ever had the honor of watching Kaori Noro play golf?" Noro held the top spot in the Sony ranking of world golfers. In the past two years, he had won the British Open and the Masters and had finished second and fourth in the U.S. Open.

"Not in person, no; only on television. But what does that have to do with destroying Pebble Beach?"

"Destroy?" Komoto asked, smiling. "Nothing will be destroyed but the golf course. The beauty of Pebble Beach will be retained, only in different form. As for Kaori, well, it is my belief that he will win on Sunday and become the *last* champion of your famous pro-am. As owner, I find that a fitting way to end."

"Noro won't win," Kevin snarled.

"Oh? And who will beat him?"

"I will."

"You?" Komoto said. "How amusing." He smiled.

"You haven't played this caliber of golf in years," Leonard said. "Besides, you're not even entered."

"A pro named Ken Fuller had to withdraw. I'll take his place. As host pro, I can do that."

Leonard shook his head. "Your *place* is in the pro shop, Kevin. Hell, you haven't played 10 times since you got here. You'd make a fool out of yourself."

"As I suspected, Mister Courtney," Komoto said. "It would be an embarrassment."

"I can beat your man."

"Highly unlikely."

His heart racing, Kevin asked, "Are you willing to make a bet on that?"

Komoto put both hands together and steepled his fingers. "I don't need your money, young man."

"No, but you do need my silence. One call by me to the media, and you'll have every golfer in America screaming for the names of the people in your syndicate. Rich people don't like that kind of bad publicity," Kevin said. "Sometimes it makes them get cold feet."

Komoto glanced at Leonard, then looked back at Kevin. "So you think you can beat the great Noro? What exactly is the bet you propose?"

"My pledge of secrecy against your pledge not to sell Pebble Beach. If I beat Noro in the tournament," Kevin said, "you'll keep Pebble Beach just the way it is. If he kicks my ass, I won't interfere with the sale."

Komoto's small black eyes had the hardness of steel. "I see little advantage in your favor, Mr. Courtney."

"Perhaps."

Speaking to Leonard but without looking at him, Komoto said, "A piece of paper, Jack."

"Mr. Komoto, I don't think ..."

"If you please," Komoto said sternly.

Kevin left the house 10 minutes later. In the inside pocket of his sport coat was a folded copy of the handwritten agreement.

His hands were trembling as he navigated the curves of 17-Mile Drive, an aftereffect of his encounter with Komoto. He also felt a knot of pressure in his stomach, the same kind of pressure that had forced him off the Tour. *Good God*, he thought. *How am I going to beat the best player in the world?* He wondered when he could squeeze in a few hours of practice, and then made a mental note to find out which of the three courses Ken Fuller had been scheduled to play on Thursday.

Oh, shit! Thursday was the day of the hearing about Joey.

Maybe they could have it moved. No, somebody—Brad or Sara—had said that the judge's calendar was booked for the next few months. That would mean May. *Damn.*

Kevin pulled the piece of paper out of his coat and set it on the passenger seat. He was fairly sure that postponing the meeting with the judge would have an effect on his chances of gaining joint custody of his son. His ex-wife would definitely hear about it and would definitely make sure the judge knew, too. How much that would hurt him, Kevin couldn't even guess. Maybe a lot, maybe a little. Maybe the judge would understand and not be so hard on him once he learned about the bet with Komoto. What was a given was that Pebble Beach Golf Links would no longer be in existence if Kevin didn't try to beat the world's best golfer. The possibility of being successful, he knew, was slim. But he had to try.

God forgive me, he thought, *and Joey, too, but I have to play.*

CHAPTER 2

The bone-chilling February wind that was blowing in from the Pacific wasn't the only reason Kevin was shivering. He hadn't been this nervous on the day he was in the final pairing at the Masters. Waiting to be announced by the starter, he looked around at the hundred or so people gathered around the first tee at Spyglass Hill GC. Many were friends who were delighted he was coming out of retirement for this one tournament. *If they only knew*, Kevin thought.

No one knew the whole story, though, not even Sara Arnold. When he called the law firm earlier, he learned that Brad was still hospitalized but doing well. He told Sara the "what"—that he couldn't make the hearing because he was playing in the tournament—but not the real why. He wanted to tell her that he wasn't just selfishly playing in a tournament, that Joey meant more to him than any round of golf, but he couldn't. Kevin, Komoto, and Leonard had pledged their secrecy.

So for five long minutes, he had listened to her argue,

plead, condemn, and cajole, until finally she sighed and said, "Okay, I'll talk to Judge Higgins."

"Thanks."

"You're making a mistake, Kevin."

He was remembering the phone conversation as he heard the starter announce, "Please welcome the host professional at Pebble Beach Golf Links, Kevin Courtney."

The introduction produced enthusiastic applause. Kevin acknowledged it with a grim nod before teeing up his ball. Fumbling fingers caused the Titleist 3 to fall off the tiny white, wooden peg and he had to re-tee. He felt himself blushing as he looked down the fairway to the ideal landing area on the 600-yard par-5 hole. His eyes needed to work as a team with his brain and muscles, locking in the swing, which would then propel the ball to its proper destination. There was no provision in this intricate process for thoughts of Joey or Masaru Komoto or Kaori Noro; nor could he be distracted by the enormously tall pine trees and the sand and scrub which awaited an errant drive.

Turn it loose, Mother Goose he thought to himself as he addressed the ball. Hopefully, this silly little rhyme would produce the tempo so necessary in golf—especially tournament golf. He took a practice swing, two deep breaths, another practice swing, then realized he wasn't ready; never would be ready. He had no right to be there, pretending he had a chance of beating the world's best golfer. At this very minute he should be in Judge Higgins's court, fighting for Joey.

Turn it loose, Mother Goose, turn it loose.

Somehow, the little ploy worked. Applause and shouts of encouragement merged with Kevin's sigh of relief as he watched the ball rocket into the wind blowing in from the Pacific and finally roll to a stop in the middle of the fairway. How many more drives like this would he need in the next four days, how many irons equally as precise, how many perfect putts?

Sara Arnold had delved into his character Monday evening. That was nothing compared to the rigorous examination that his character and his golf swing would face out here over the next four days.

The tournament was the only one of its kind on the PGA Tour. It pitted 180 teams, each consisting of a professional and an amateur, against Spyglass Hill, Cypress Point, and Pebble Beach. On Sunday, the low 25 teams and the low 60 pros would play Pebble to determine both the team and individual champions.

An hour earlier, Kevin had been hitting balls on the practice tee when heard a loud voice call, "Kevin Courtney?"

The man resembled a peacock: lavender slacks and shirt and a pink sweater. White alligator shoes completed the costume. He was on the short side, and a few years younger than Kevin. "Right here. Are you my amateur?"

"Larry Caldwell." The man put up his hand for a high five. "Let's go get 'em, Kev. We're going to win this mother."

Kevin smiled and raised his hand to accept his partner's greeting. "Glad to meet you, Larry."

"They say you won on the Tour and now you're the main man around here. Got four more good rounds in you, pro?"

"I hope so," Kevin murmured, returning to work. His 5-iron raked a ball from the pile of glistening white Titleists. Thinking only of his rhythm, he struck it pure. Caldwell watched him hit several more textbook shots.

"Awesome, man! We're gonna win this mother," he repeated, taking a ball from Kevin's pile and teeing it up.

"See what you think of this action." After at least a dozen waggles, he dribbled the Titleist off the tee. "Shit." Caldwell reached for another ball.

"Larry, if I'm going to be any help to this team, I need to use all of these. Right over there you can get your own balls."

"You mean my caddie can," Caldwell replied. "When you have as much money as I do, you don't get your own *anything*."

Now, walking down the first fairway, Kevin's partner was explaining how he struck it rich. "The Silicon Valley, man. That's where it's at. Five years ago, I was a nobody in a metallurgical lab. Then I met this genius in a bar who said he had a fantastic software program. All he needed, he said, was 'venture capital.' Hell, I didn't even know what venture capital was. But when he started talking about numbers with lots of zeros after them, I figured I'd better find out. I did, and was on the way to my first million." Slapping Kevin on the back, he added, "You know what they say, Kev, the first million is the hardest."

"Right," Kevin said, wondering how Larry got an invitation to play in the tournament and vowing not to let his antics interfere with his concentration. But something—perhaps thinking of Larry's hollering after a surprisingly good second shot or perhaps being unsure because he hadn't hit his 2-iron all that much or perhaps simply the pressure of the situation—caused him to push the long iron into the trees.

Blocking him from his target some 165 yards away was a pine tree. A 6-iron with a big draw might catch the right corner of the elevated, bunkered green. But the wind was gusting from the left. If he'd had Mike on his bag, his former regular Tour caddie, he would have consulted with him. He'd tried to get him for the tournament, but Mike was now working for another player. So he'd had to settle for Bruce, the caddie who had been assigned to Ken Fuller. Kevin knew the three courses pretty well; all he expected from Bruce was for the youngster to carry his clubs and stay out of the way.

He took the 6-iron, addressed the ball, backed off, thought for a second, and finally exchanged the mid-iron for a pitching wedge. He would try to place it around 100 yards from the green and see if he could make par from there.

"Go for it, Kev!" Caldwell shouted suddenly. "You see my last two shots? I got us covered for the par."

Startled, Kevin stared at his partner.

"Let's kick ass on the first damn hole!" the peacock cried.

Kevin walked halfway over. "How long have you been playing golf, Larry?"

"Four or five years, probably."

"I have 20 years on you. How about I let you know if I need your advice?"

"Jesus," Caldwell muttered, backing away.

Miraculously, despite the interruption, Kevin got his par after his sand wedge fourth shot rolled to within six feet of the hole and he made the putt. Without extending to his fellow competitors the courtesy of waiting for them to putt out, Larry was on his way to the next tee.

No surprise. He typified a new breed of golfers that didn't concern itself with golf etiquette or traditions. On the first tee, it was possible for these golfers to be mistaken for tour players with their thousand-dollar wardrobes and huge golf bags filled with the latest high-tech equipment. But the illusion was shattered the moment they lurched at the ball. Many critics thought that golf carts were the reason, because they removed much of the athleticism from golf. On the other hand, golf carts also brought the masses to the game, and their revenue helped pay the salaries of club pros like Kevin. Still, he longed for the days when there were more caddies than carts or players used pull-carts or carried their clubs.

Watching Caldwell standing on the tee, shoulders slumped, Kevin shook his head. The year after he'd been runner-up at Augusta, he'd been paired with the actor James Garner. *There* was a class act. Now he was stuck with a partner who was behaving like a spoiled child. But then, did it really matter? Sighing, Kevin realized it did. Golf provided its own conflicts, and this week they were being multiplied by Komoto and Joey. He didn't need the added burden of clashing with his partner. After the final putt dropped, Kevin walked rapidly to the second tee and put an arm around Caldwell's shoulder.

"Sorry I growled at you, Larry. Let's play some golf."

"Sure."

"I mean it. You swing better than a 16 handicap. I think we'll do all right."

Caldwell looked at him. "Really? You like my swing"

"You've got a pretty good move."

"I played semipro baseball for two years," Caldwell said brightly. He made a practice swing. "Where I lose it is around the greens. You know?"

"Maybe I can help you, if you don't mind a tip or two."

"Lay it on me, man. I came here to win."

He played like it on the second hole. At Kevin's suggestion, he used his putter instead of the wedge from four feet off the green and got it down in two for his par. Because of his handicap, which allowed him to subtract a stroke on all but the third and fifteenth holes, it meant he had produced a net birdie for the team. It also produced another high five.

The next three holes at Spyglass weave through sand dunes along the Pacific Ocean. After battling the wind for a par on the second hole, Kevin looked at the bowed flagstick on the 150-yard third. He debated between a 6- or 7-iron before punching the longer club below the worst of the wind and somehow stopped it 10 feet from the hole. Twice, addressing the putt, he had to step away to regain his balance. He widened his stance still further and hunkered down over the ball. He then made a solid stroke and watched the windblown Titleist wobble into the low side of the hole. It put him one under par.

The thunder of giant waves crashing on the rocky coast below the fourth tee confirmed the wind's ferocity. An even-par 72 would be a good score considering the conditions. Pebble Beach and Cypress Point were even less protected than Spyglass. All three courses would produce high numbers today—and many frustrated golfers.

Kevin wondered if one of them would be Kaori Noro. The Japanese star was playing Cypress, scheduled to tee off in a few minutes. Kevin told himself not to think about Noro. He had decided not to look at the leader board, too. There was nothing he could do about what Noro did, so why worry about it? Just play your own game.

Kevin made par on the fourth and fifth holes but they weren't pretty. The one at four was due to a dying-gasp putt that somehow fell in; the one at five was the result of a bladed chip shot that slammed into the flagstick and stopped inches away. Some rounds were like that, with more luck than skill involved. Kevin didn't expect it to continue but he hoped it would.

It did. After the first five holes, which are played along the shore's dunes, the par-4 sixth at Spyglass climbs up into the woods. The dogleg to the right measured 415 yards. Kevin hit a 1-iron to the left center of the fairway, then hit a nice 7-iron that stopped 15 feet below the hole. He made the putt.

The peacock was playing the front nine very well, too. Another net birdie on the eighth hole made him as excited as a kid on Christmas Day.

"Hell, Kevin, using my putter instead of that dumb wedge is the best tip I ever got. No way we're going to lose this mother!"

After routine pars on seven and eight—in spite of Larry's enthusiasm and improved conduct—Kevin stood on the ninth tee thinking that the only thing that mattered about the team score was that it didn't interfere with his own play. He somehow had to beat Noro.

His reward for this loss of concentration was a snap-hook into the woods. Miraculously, the ball ricocheted back to the middle of the fairway. "Thanks," Kevin murmured, lifting his eyes to the gods of golf and vowing to shut out everything but positive golf thoughts.

He made par at nine, and then did the same at 10 and 11. The 12th hole at Spyglass is a 180-yard par 3 that's patterned after the famed Redan hole at North Berwick in Scotland. The canted green is wedged between water on the left and a bunkered rise on the right. Lou Jackson, the other professional in the group, played first, striking a magnificent shot to within three feet of the hole.

"Awesome!" Kevin's caddie shouted. "What'd you hit there?"

Kevin looked at Bruce in disbelief. "Son, you can't...oh, my God." He put his face in his hands because the kid had just cost him a two-stroke penalty. Golf's eighth rule stated that a player or his caddie could not ask another player which club he'd used on a shot.

When Kevin looked up, Bruce was staring ahead at the green.

Lou Jackson was slowly shaking his head.

"Give me a minute," Kevin said.

"Take your time," Jackson said. "I understand."

No you don't, Kevin thought. *You have no idea.* No way could he give the world's best golfer a two-stroke advantage and expect to beat him. Because of Bruce's blunder, Kevin's birdies on three and six were wiped out.

After composing himself as well as he could, Kevin pulled out his 5-iron and knocked the ball onto the center of the green. He walked to the par-3 with his head bowed, then two-putted for a double-bogey five. In spite of the turmoil raging within him, he also managed to par the 13th.

The 555-yard par-5 14th at Spyglass is a double-dogleg. Kevin played it to perfection, pitching his third shot to within five feet and then stroking the birdie putt dead center. His insides, though, continued to churn. He was one under par again, and at worst, he had to stay there.

On the tee of the short par-3 15th, Larry said, "What do you think, pro?"

"Nice, smooth eight," Kevin replied.

Moments later, Larry was yelling, "Go in!" Then, "Damn!" when the ball barely missed the flagstick and rolled several feet beyond. "I guess we'll have to settle for a deuce, Kev."

Larry was clearly thinking positively, greedy for more. Kevin was doing the opposite, hoping to maintain what he had. He tried to change his mind-set at the green, but stupidly left his birdie attempt short. He did it again on 16.

A short dogleg left of only 320 yards, the 17th could possibly allow Kevin to get back to two under par and maybe shoot a 70. *Be positive*, he thought. But the branches lining the fairway were thousands of giant arms eagerly waiting to grab his ball. Having to wait on the group ahead didn't help. He turned his back on the hole as the wind whistling through the trees ruffled his blond hair and carried an aromatic mixture of saltwater, seaweed, and pine needles.

He forced his mind to forget the giant arms, to think instead of an article he had seen in that morning's newspaper. It was a report on the writer Robert Louis Stevenson. He had lived in the Del Monte Forest over a hundred years earlier, and the area had given him the inspiration to write *Treasure Island*. The name of the golf course he was now playing, Spyglass Hill, had been inspired by the novel.

Kevin's fellow pro interrupted his thoughts. "They're out of the way now."

"Okay." He had already pulled the 1-iron from his bag. He took a practice swing...and a divot. *Tempo, Kevin.* Following two more practice swings and a deep breath, he managed to steer the ball clear of the grasping branches. A smooth pitching wedge left an eight-footer for birdie.

Larry, standing in a greenside bunker preparing to hit his third shot, impressed Kevin with his preparation. He opened his stance and the clubface of his sand wedge, then twisted his feet until they were anchored firmly. It was possible that only Kevin saw him brush the sand when he took the club back.

The ball floated out of the bunker on a cushion of sand and rolled to within inches of the hole. Larry raised a clenched fist and flashed a broad grin. Kevin stared at his partner and wondered if he had even realized what he had done. Could it be possible that the guy really didn't know that you're not allowed to touch the sand with your club before you make a shot from a bunker? Didn't every golfer know that?

"Kevin, how 'bout that?" Larry shouted.

"Great shot, Larry," Kevin said. "But I'm afraid you touched the sand on your backswing."

"What?"

"You touched the sand on your backswing."

"No freaking way."

Kevin pointed to a small furrow behind the spot where the wedge had dug into the sand. "Sorry, but it's a two-stroke penalty."

Caldwell stared at Kevin with his mouth open but no words came out. He looked at the other two players but they just shrugged; they hadn't been in a position to see what happened. Larry walked quickly to his ball, knocked it off the green with his club, then turned around and glared at Kevin. "You self-righteous asshole," he said.

After watching Larry stomp off to the next tee, Kevin tried to compose himself and make the birdie putt. The attempt to calm down was useless. When he could stall no longer, he jabbed the ball three feet beyond the hole. Fortunately, he caught enough of the lip on his next putt to save par.

Walking to the 18th tee, Kevin tried to get his thinking back on track. Even without Larry's temper tantrum, his nerves or a poor read of the line might have caused him to miss the putt. *Forget about 17. You're still one under par. Keep it going.* He teed up his ball by the right marker on the 405-yard hole, then stood behind it and pictured hitting it with a slight fade. He saw exactly where it would land. Unlike at the previous hole, anger replaced fear and he was able to block out the trees that seemed to reach into the fairway from both sides. He took a practice swing, settled in over the ball, pulled the club back and was into his downswing when Caldwell coughed.

The flinch that resulted caused him to catch the ball in the heel. It headed for the woods to the right. Kevin watched until it disappeared in branches, then looked around to find Larry. His partner was on his way to the forward tee that was used by the amateurs. Kevin caught up with him.

"That's the first time I heard you cough all day, Larry," he whispered. "Even if you really had to, you should have tried to hold it long enough for me to complete my swing. That kind of behavior, *partner*, has no place on a golf course. Got that?"

Without waiting for a response, Kevin veered off in the direction his ball had taken. Once again, he would have to try to calm down. Maybe the trees wouldn't be that dense. Maybe there'd be an opening and he could still make par.

But then, maybe not.

When he found his ball, Kevin saw that he was blocked by a giant pine tree. The flagstick was set in the right front corner of the green, stuck behind a deep bunker. He studied the situation and wondered if he could hit a big cut with a 6-iron and maybe catch the left side of the putting surface. He looked up again and saw Caldwell and his caddie walking past the green, heading for the clubhouse.

Refocusing, Kevin wondered if he should take the risk of hitting the tree and a possible big score. Unconsciously, he glanced at his caddie for advice. *Hell, the kid hadn't even apologized for what had happened on 12.* Kevin wished he had Mike with him to provide some much-needed confidence.

Playing it safe, he could advance the ball to within a hundred yards of the green—a comfortable yardage for his sand wedge. Reluctantly, he pitched the ball up the fairway. His wedge to the green, however, was uninspired. The 20-footer for par missed on the low side and Kevin had to settle for a bogey.

Leaving the green, Kevin glanced around but didn't see his so-called "partner." To his surprise, though, he did see some-one totally unexpected: Sara Arnold. She was looking at a leader board. Kevin wondered if she was looking to see if his name was on it; it wasn't. But Noro's was. After 15 holes at Cypress, he was four under par.

A possible 68, in this wind? Kevin shook his head. Four shots down to the best golfer in the world—after only the first day—would be tough to make up.

He returned his attention to his attorney. He hadn't noticed her in any of the small groups of spectators out on the golf course. Was she looking for him for some reason?

Or was she maybe here to watch one of the other players?

CHAPTER 3

Before he went inside the small scorer's tent off the 18th green, Kevin got Sara's attention and waved at her. Inside at the table, he checked the scorecard and verified a 66 for the team of Courtney and Caldwell. That is, if it still existed. He then verified his own even-par 72, shaking his head at the double-bogey on 12 before signing his name to make it official.

Leaving the tent, Kevin walked over to where his caddie Bruce was standing with his clubs. Sara was waiting nearby. "I won't be needing you anymore," Kevin said. He handed the caddie 40 dollars—much more than he felt he deserved.

"Fine," Bruce said sullenly. "What do you want me to do with the clubs?"

"Leave them here."

Bruce left the bag standing upright and hurried away.

"Don't need him anymore?" Sara asked, walking over. "You quitting?"

"No, I fired him. I'll have to get a new caddie, if I can find one."

"Why'd you fire him?"

"He cost me a two-stroke penalty."

"How?"

"He asked another player what club he used."

"You can't do that, huh?"

"Nope."

"What did you shoot?"

"Even par 72."

"That's good," Sara said. "Isn't it?"

"Could've been better."

"What's better?"

Kevin pointed at the leader board. "See that red four after the name 'Noro'? It means he's four *under* par. *That's* better."

"Oh."

"Since you're obviously not a golf fan, Sara," Kevin said smiling, "what're you doing out here?"

"Judge Higgins called me about an hour and a half ago," she said. "An attorney who had a hearing scheduled for tomorrow had a death in the family. Higgins can hear our case at 1:00."

Kevin shook his head. "Won't do me any good; I'm playing in the pro-am again tomorrow. What I need is an opening next week."

"It's possible, of course," Sara said, "but unlikely. If you don't grab the one tomorrow, it'll probably be three months before we can get in front of the judge. I'm sure you know what I think you should do."

Kevin turned his head and looked down the 18th fairway. Spyglass Hill was definitely a great place to play. As was Cypress Point...and the Olympic Club in San Francisco...and Riviera in Los Angeles. Maybe Komoto was right; maybe one less course wouldn't make that much difference.

More to the point, was there anything that Kevin could do about it anyhow? He looked at the leader board and saw that Kaori had bogeyed 16. Take away the two-stroke penalty, and the strokes that Larry Caldwell helped him lose on 17 and 18, and Kevin would actually be one stroke ahead at this point.

"I have to call the court and let them know if we're going to take the opening," Sara said. "What do you think?"

"I have to work tomorrow."

"You have to play *golf* tomorrow."

"Golf professionals play golf for money," Kevin said. "That's how we make our living. It's how we pay our attorneys."

"The way you were talking Monday night," Sara said, "I was under the impression that you couldn't *wait* to get joint custody of your son."

Kevin started to respond but stopped.

"Perhaps I was wrong. Perhaps you don't want Joey as much as I thought."

"That's not true."

"It's not?" Sara asked. "Well, good. You have a chance to prove it by going to the hearing tomorrow."

"I can't," Kevin said. "And I can't explain it."

He heard someone call his name and turned around to see a Tour official standing behind him. "They're asking for you in the Media Center. I'll take you over when you're ready to go."

"The writers want to hear about my sizzling 72? Why?"

"They want to ask you about your penalty and what happened with your partner."

"Ancient history."

"I'm afraid not, Kevin," the man said. "You may need to do some damage control."

"Damage control? The only damage there was, was done

to me."

"Then you need to explain it. It's your obligation as the head pro here"

"All right, give me a minute."

He took Sara's arm and gently guided her out of hearing range of the official. "Sara, listen. Thanks for coming all the way out here. I'm sorry that it was a waste of your time."

Arms folded and her head cocked to one side, she stared at him for several seconds. "Like I told you on Tuesday, Kevin, you're making a mistake. A big mistake." She pulled her arm out of his hand, turned around and walked away.

A jeweler, pharmacy, sportswear store, art gallery, gift shop, and beauty salon are among the first-floor tenants in a complex on the other side of the putting green from The Lodge. On the second floor, there was a Conference Center that was being utilized by the media. Kevin sat on a raised platform beside Richard Gardner, the Tour's Communications Director.

"Anything you want to tell us about your round?" Gardner asked.

"I played pretty well for not having played much," Kevin said. "Obviously, the wind made the ocean holes more difficult. If it hadn't been for a penalty on 12..."

"Tell us about that."

"Not much to say," Kevin said, leaning back in his chair. "After the other pro in the group, Lou Jackson, hit his tee shot, my caddie, for some reason, asked him what club he used."

A dozen or so media people were seated in front of the platform. Kevin recognized several of them. One unwelcome face was that of Dean Adams, a local reporter he'd ordered off the course a few weeks before for gouging a chunk out of the first green after missing a putt.

"Wasn't he an experienced caddie?" someone asked.

"Supposed to be."

"Will he be caddying for you tomorrow?"

"No."

"You fired him because of one mistake?" Adams asked.

"I fired him because of one *big* mistake," Kevin answered.

"Was that before or after you made your partner quit?"

Kevin sat up straight. "I didn't make him quit. He picked up his ball and walked off."

"Didn't you tell him he didn't belong on a golf course?"

"No. I said certain types of behavior didn't belong on a golf course."

"Such as?"

"It was a private conversation."

Hank Fellows, a reporter for *Golf World* and a longtime acquaintance, spoke up. "As I understand it, your amateur partner stormed off the course without playing the 18th."

"That's true."

"Something happen that ticked him off?"

"There was a question as to whether he had accidentally touched the sand in a bunker on 17."

"What you're saying is, you accused him of cheating," Adams said.

Kevin's thoughts flashed back to when he was eleven years old and the pro at his course asked him to play nine holes. They rode together in a cart. Although nervous, Kevin was eager to show off his game. He needed par on the last hole to break 40 for the first time. His tee shot ended up in the rough. Getting ready to hit his 5-iron, he watched in horror as the ball moved. The movement had been barely perceptible, but Kevin saw it. When he glanced at the cart, the pro was looking toward the green.

"What did you have there, Kevin?" the pro asked when they finished the hole.

"A par."

"I'm afraid you didn't, son," the pro said. "Both of us saw the ball move, didn't we?"

Kevin dropped his head.

"In every round, there are opportunities to cheat," the pro said. "The thing that makes golf so special is that most people play by the rules." The pro put an arm around Kevin's shoulders. "They do it because they have respect for the game of golf, and for themselves." He squeezed Kevin's shoulder before driving to the clubhouse. "You played a fine round, Kevin."

For a long time Kevin sat alone, too ashamed to go in the pro shop to drop off his clubs and get his tennis shoes. He ended up walking the six blocks home in his golf shoes and carrying his clubs. He didn't go to the course for three days. His buddies would know. Everyone would know. But when a couple of friends called and didn't say anything about cheating, for the first time Kevin dared to hope the pro hadn't told anyone. And apparently he hadn't, because no one ever mentioned it.

"Kevin?" Gardner said, raising his eyebrows.

The last person in the world Kevin owed a favor to was Larry Caldwell. But the club pro hadn't owed anything to the eleven-year-old boy, either. "I didn't accuse him of *cheating*. I simply pointed out to him that he had accidentally touched the sand. Any pro would've done the same thing."

Adams's eyes hardened, as did the lips above his red goatee. "Then why didn't he finish his round?"

"I don't know. Why don't you ask *him*?"

"I did. He said you told him he didn't belong in the tournament."

"Then he must've misunderstood me."

"Tell us your exact words."

"Look, I've already told you that it was a private conversation," Kevin said. "That's all I have to say about the whole thing." He looked around the room. "Any other questions?"

"How did it feel being back in competition after laying off for so long?" Fellows asked.

"There were a few cobwebs, in my brain and in my swing. Fortunately, I was able to get rid of them and play a halfway respectable round."

Kevin answered a few more routine questions before turning to Gardner. "Sorry, but I have get back to the pro shop."

The Pebble Beach pro shop is a paradise for golf shoppers. Even when there wasn't a tournament, golfers and tourists jammed the aisles to buy anything with the distinctive Pebble Beach logo on it: caps, visors, hats, sweaters, windbreakers, shirts, towels, headcovers, bag tags, key chains, golf balls, ball markers, divot tools. This being the first day of the pro-am, it was even more of a zoo and Kevin had to squeeze through the enthusiastic buyers. Thankfully, no one stopped him to chat or to ask about his round as he headed for the security of his office.

The clock on his desk read 5:10. No doubt Sara had long since notified the court that he couldn't make it the next day. He told himself it was the right decision—the only possible decision. Still, he flashed on Joey's face as he picked up the phone and punched in the caddiemaster's telephone number. It was answered immediately.

"Ernie, I need your help."

"Goodness, Kevin, I heard about your difficulties." Ernest

Goodwin, a retired minister, had been in charge of the caddies for five years. "You'll require someone for the remainder of the tournament."

"Someone who has a clue what he's doing, Ernie."

"I must say you've given me a mountain to climb," Goodwin said. "All the good ones have been taken by the amateurs. I don't...wait a minute. It just came to me like a message from above. Willie Strath."

Kevin waited.

"I don't know if Willie would do it. He hasn't caddied since his son passed away, but he would be an asset. Actually, I'm not certain that he's still around. Perhaps not. Let me examine all of my cards and see if there is anyone else..."

"Tell me about this Willie person."

"Yes. Willie Strath. Came over from Scotland about two years ago."

"You said he had a son. How old is this Willie Strath?"

The caddiemaster chuckled. "That is a relative term, Kevin. Older than the other caddies. Younger than I."

"How old, Ernie?"

"Approaching sixty, perhaps."

"Go on."

"Willie used to caddie at St. Andrews, and some other famous Scottish courses that I can't recall. You would probably recognize their names. He resided with his son in Pacific Grove. I believe he caddied at Cypress Point before coming here. Less than a year after he arrived, his boy died. His son was an artist—painter—as I understand it."

"Go on."

"I fear I have exhausted my repertoire on Willie Strath."

"You said he hasn't caddied since his boy died. How long

ago was that?"

"My memory says nine months," Goodwin said. "Of course, he might have gone back to Cypress Point or on to another course. Let me examine his card for verification."

St. Andrews. Kevin drummed his fingers on his wooden desktop.

"Goodness gracious, Kevin, I amaze myself sometimes. Nine months to the date."

"I'm proud of you. What's his phone number?"

"My memory says...but let me examine the card to be sure. Yes, I'm right; he doesn't have a telephone."

"Figures."

"Patience is still a virtue, my boy. I do have the address."

Kevin jotted down Walnut Street and the numbers Goodwin gave him, then stared at the piece of notepaper. *Willie Strath.* With the tournament traffic, it would take a good half-hour to get there. Strath might be gone, working somewhere—probably was gone if he hadn't been around Pebble for nine months. Surely Kevin had more important things to do than run off on some wild-goose chase.

The other notation on the piece of paper caught his eye again. *St. Andrews.* That's what Kevin kept seeing as he walked out to the 18th tee later: St. Andrews. It was the only place that he held in more reverence than Pebble Beach. If Willie Strath had caddied at St. Andrews and Pebble Beach and Cypress Point, he must be something special.

Upon reaching the tee, Kevin immediately turned around and walked back. Fifteen minutes later, he was driving past the polo field that was now being used as a practice range. There must have been 40 players in a firing line stretching almost a hundred yards. Each was hoping to groove what had worked earlier in the day or to fix what hadn't.

That's where you should be Kevin, thought. *Not driving out to Pacific Grove.* Even if it turned out that there wasn't a Willie Strath, though, he needed to focus for a few stress-free minutes on nothing more threatening than the 17-Mile Drive's rocky coastline. The deer and sea lions, the palatial estates, the pine and cypress forests.

Five minutes later the ring of his car phone was an unwelcome interruption. "Hello."

"Kevin?"

He thought he recognized the feminine voice. "Yeah."

"This is Sara." Before he could respond, she added, "You can cool your jets. This isn't about the hearing."

"Good."

"I meant to call you sooner, but I've been with a client ever since I got back to the office. Anyhow, something happened that I thought you should know about."

"What's that?"

"When I came out to the course this afternoon, I managed to get into the VIP parking lot. There was a fender-bender near the entrance, so the police had to reroute traffic and I just sort of drove in."

"Interesting move for an attorney."

"You want interesting?" Sara asked. "After I left you, I came back to my car. As I was leaving the lot, I saw your caddie; that kid you fired. He was standing by a tree, kind of hiding but at the same time looking around. Like he was waiting for someone, to get picked up or something. So anyhow, this car drives up and your caddie comes out to meet it. As I said, like he was getting a ride. But instead of him getting in, this hand comes out of the driver-side window with an envelope in it. Letter-size, it looked like. The kid takes the envelope, the car drives off, and the kid walks through the parking lot and eventually out of my sight."

"Sounds like a scene from a spy movie," Kevin said.

"Actually," Sara said, "it was more like I was watching footage from a surveillance camera, you know? Like the film of a drug buy."

"Huh. Pretty strange."

"Very. I mean, I saw you pay him, right?"

"Yeah, I paid him," Kevin said. "He didn't deserve what I gave him, but he got it anyhow."

"Well, that's what's so troubling about what I saw."

"What do you mean?

"Obviously, I can't say for sure," Sara said, "but I had the distinct impression that there was money in that envelope."

Kevin told her to hang on while he found a place to pull off the road. He saw a scenic overlook up ahead, turned in and parked the car.

"You're sure it was Bruce?"

"If that's your caddie's name, then yeah."

"Could you see who gave him the envelope?"

"No, the windows were tinted and I was at an angle from the rear."

"Could you tell if the person was Oriental?"

"No," Sara said. "All I saw was an arm, a hand, and an envelope."

"What kind of car?"

"Small, dark blue Chevy. Cavalier, maybe. A four-door."

"You get the license number?"

"No, there was a parked car in the way."

"You think there was money in the envelope?"

"I said I had the *impression* there was money in it."

"Did Bruce open it right away?"

"No, he put it in his back pocket and took off."

When Kevin didn't respond, she said, "You told me your caddie did something stupid and you were penalized for it. What'd he do?"

After he explained it, Sara said, "Is that unusual, to break that rule?"

"Yeah, it is," Kevin replied. "I mean, a brand-new caddie might do something like that, but not an experienced one. And if Bruce had been brand-new, the caddiemaster never would have assigned him to a pro. A caddie who doesn't know what he's doing can cost you some money."

"It might also be a way for him to *make* some money, too," Sara said.

Kevin's eyes hardened.

"Can you think of anybody who might have *paid* him to make that mistake?"

"Bribed him, you mean?"

"Bribed him."

Yeah, I can, Kevin thought suddenly. *A couple of people.*

"Shit," he said.

"What?"

"Nothin'."

"Why'd you say 'shit'?"

"No reason."

"Why'd you ask me if the person in the car was Oriental?"

"I don't know, just wondering."

"I found that question very curious, Kevin, " Sara said. "*Very* curious."

"Forget about it," Kevin said. "I don't even know why I

asked."

"Sure you do, you're just not telling me. I mean, you postpone for a whole three months the chance to see your son more often, just so you can play in a *golf* tournament? You've probably played in *hundreds* of golf tournaments," Sara said. "What makes this one so special? There's something going on besides the pro-am, isn't there, Kevin? Talk to me."

Kevin didn't say anything.

"Somebody pays your caddie to do something that will get you penalized," Sara said. "*You* wonder if it was an Oriental. Is that because you're a bigot, Kevin, or because you know something that you're not telling me about?" She paused. "Wait a second. Isn't Pebble Beach owned by a Japanese guy?"

"Yeah, so?"

"So...if there's something going on that may affect the hearing..."

"Stop right there," Kevin said quickly. "You said this call wasn't going to be about the hearing."

Sara paused again. When she finally did speak, her tone was icy. "Yes, you're right. I did say that. Sorry to have bothered you, Mr. Courtney."

The line went dead.

Kevin sighed and hung up the phone. He regretted pissing her off, but he was glad the conversation had ended. She was getting too close to figuring out some things. He also needed to make a call. One minute later, he was identifying himself to the caddiemaster at Spyglass Hill.

"I'm really sorry about what happened today," the caddiemaster said. "Bruce should have known better."

"Is he still around, Bob?"

"Hang on, I'll find out."

Kevin looked toward the ocean and the angry surf. Hundreds of brown pelicans darkened the huge rock formations that sat just offshore.

Returning to the phone, the caddiemaster said, "No, Kevin, apparently he's left."

"Have you got his phone number or address."

"Yeah, somewhere. Let me look."

Kevin heard desk drawers opening and closing. The caddiemaster said, "I understand that Bruce won't be caddying for you the rest of the tournament."

"That's true."

"Well, then ...?"

"I was a little steamed after the round," Kevin told him. "I'd like to apologize."

"What're you going to do for a caddie tomorrow?"

"I found another one."

"Well, that's good," Bob said. "Here it is, Kevin. Got a pencil?"

Kevin had regained his composure by the time he got back onto 17-Mile Drive. Could it have been one of Komoto's people in the Cavalier? He smiled at the thought that the owner of Pebble Beach might actually be worrying that Kevin would beat the best player in the world. The smile didn't last, though. When he'd signed the agreement, the odds that he would win were probably a-thousand-to-one. How astronomical were they now, after his caddie had cost him two strokes?

Perhaps a more important question was, what could an old Scotsman do about it?

CHAPTER 4

Kevin turned off the highway on the outskirts of the small town on the tip of the Monterey Peninsula. He soon found Walnut Street and began reading house numbers. The address he was looking for was attached to a white board-and-batten cottage with a white picket fence. He parked in front and went up the curving stone walk; in a front window, a curtain moved. When his knocks went unanswered, he looked toward the window where the curtain had moved and saw a face. It was gone in a moment.

"Mr. Strath?" Kevin called out. "Willie Strath?"

Seconds later, the door began to slowly open. Kevin found himself facing an older man with a hooked nose, deeply etched cheeks, and sand-colored eyes beneath bushy, white eyebrows. The man's hair, as white as his eyebrows, was untamed. Kevin knew he had never seen this face before, yet something about it was strangely familiar.

"Sir, are you Willie Strath?"

"Aye."

Although he wasn't a large man, Strath exuded a certain strength—both physical and mental. If first impressions meant anything, Kevin decided the old caddie might be an asset. "My name is Kevin Courtney. I'm the head professional at Pebble Beach. I wonder if I could talk with you for a minute."

The man's lips compressed into a thin line, neither a smile nor a frown. He nodded once.

Kevin hesitated, wondering if there was a good way to break the ice. Nothing came to him. "Mr. Strath, I'm playing in the Pebble Beach National Pro-Am. The caddie I had today cost me a two-stroke penalty. I need a new one, and I've been told that you've very good at it. Would you be interested in taking the job?"

A softening of the old man's mouth gave Kevin a glimpse of hope.

"I play at Pebble tomorrow at 11:00."

"No, I'm sorry," Strath said. "I cannot do that."

"Sir, I'm not just a club pro. I won three times on the Tour before taking the position at Pebble. I got into the field at the last minute, but I'm hittin' it good. And it's very important that I do well this week. To do that, though, I need a good caddie."

"I hope you are successful, lad," the man said. "But I'm afraid I can't help you."

"But, sir, everybody says..."

"I no longer wish to caddie."

"...that you're one of the best." Strath didn't hear the last part of Kevin's plea; he had closed the door.

Kevin stared at the barrier between him and Willie Strath. Why had he thought this might work, when nothing else that day had? Halfway to his car, he stopped suddenly. The old man's sand-colored eyes were just like his father's. Kevin was only six when his dad was killed in an automobile accident, so he didn't remember too much about him. But he could remember the gentleness of his eyes. In spite of the Scotsman's refusal, his eyes had that same look. Another thing: over the old guy's shoulder, Kevin had seen a painting above the fireplace. There was something about that picture...

Kevin turned back toward the house.

The door opened before he had a chance to knock, almost as if his return was expected. "I apologize for bothering you again, Mr. Strath, but I'd appreciate it if you'd reconsider. I desperately need your help."

"Who sent you here?"

"Ernie Goodwin."

"He's a good man," Strath said, and again his mouth softened. "I'm sorry if you've wasted your time. I'm no longer interested in caddying."

Kevin pointed to the large spotlighted seascape over the fireplace. "Did your son paint that?"

"Aye," he whispered, slowly turning around.

"It's beautiful. May I see it?"

Wordlessly, Strath stepped aside. Kevin approached the painting, a depiction of the 17-Mile Drive's "Lone Cypress Tree," clinging to a rocky cliff just out of reach of the foaming surf. In the lower right corner was a small signature: *I. Strath*.

"It's magnificent," Kevin said.

"Aye, 'tis," the old man said. He walked over and stood beside Kevin in front of the fireplace.

"None of the photographs of the tree that I've seen, ever captured it like this," Kevin said. "Fragile, but at the same time powerful...stronger than even the wind or the ocean. It reaches right out into the room."

"Aye."

The two men looked at the painting in silence until Willie asked, "Did Ernest tell you about my son?"

"Only that you lost him recently," Kevin said. "I'm sorry."

"Ian had so much talent...so much to give."

Kevin nodded. "You must have been proud, watching him create something this beautiful."

Strath's response was a long time coming. When it came, it was so hushed that Kevin had to strain to hear it. "I was in Scotland when he painted it."

"How long have you been in America?"

"Less than two years. I only came when..." Strath paused for a moment and composed himself. "You said your name is Courtney?"

"Yes, sir. Kevin Courtney."

"Would like a cup of coffee, lad?"

"I would, thank you."

Kevin followed him into the kitchen. He felt guilty for using the painting to get to Willie, but his praise of Ian's work was sincere.

Two seascapes framed a small window overlooking a garden. The kitchen's white vinyl floor looked clean enough to eat off, and the sink and countertop appeared spotless. Kevin smiled to himself; he had yet to meet a good caddie who wasn't fastidious about neatness.

"Black?" Strath asked.

"Yes, thank you."

"Please sit down."

Kevin took a chair at the brown wooden table. The top was covered with streaks and splotches of paint. Ian had worked at this table so it probably held a special place in his father's heart. The Scotsman filled two mugs from a pot on the stove and set them on floral placemats. As he sipped the strong, hot liquid, Kevin became aware of his host staring at him over the top of his own mug.

"How old are you, lad?"

"Thirty-two."

"Aye," Strath said nodding. "The same as Ian."

Kevin didn't know what to say, whether he should ask more questions about Ian. It was obvious his intrusion had rekindled difficult memories. "How long did you caddie at St. Andrews?"

"For no more than a year. Most of my time was spent at Carnoustie."

"I don't suppose you saw Watson win The Open there in '75?"

"Aye, lad, that I did." The sand-colored eyes seemed to twinkle. "I looped for him."

Kevin's eyebrows raised. "You were caddying for him when he won at Carnoustie?"

"Aye."

Kevin regarded the little man across the table from him in wonderment. *I'll be damned, Tom Watson's caddie.*

When Kevin was growing up, Watson was his idol. He once hitchhiked 200 miles to watch him play; he'd also majored in psychology at Stanford largely because Watson had done the same. During his PGA Tour days, Kevin had been paired with his hero a couple of times and nothing had happened to alter his high regard for the man. He still held in awe the golfer whose credits included five British Open Championships. And the man who carried his bag in one of those victories was sitting across from him.

"Did you work for Watson in any other Open?"

"Only Carnoustie."

Only Carnoustie. As if it lessened it somehow. Trying not to stare at his host, Kevin was convinced even more that he needed this man's help at Pebble Beach. He had to find a way to break through the barrier that the Scotsman had apparently erected after his son died. The question was, how?

"What course did you play today, lad?"

Kevin stared at him, his heart suddenly beating faster. "Spyglass Hill."

"And your caddie's mistake?"

Kevin told him what had happened at the par 3.

"What was your score on the hole?"

"Five."

"You did well to maintain your composure."

"*Regain* it is probably more accurate."

Strath smiled. "Aye." He pushed his chair back and walked to the window that overlooked the garden. Kevin sensed that Willie was considering the caddie job, but he was afraid of pushing the Scotsman too hard. He watched and waited.

Finally, Strath turned back to him. "What time do you want me there tomorrow, lad?"

"You'll do it?"

"Aye. Perhaps it's time I got on with my life."

Kevin stood up and put both hands on the Scotsman's shoulders. "Thank you. I know we'll make a good team."

As he drove away from Pacific Grove, Kevin's happiness about securing Willie's services was tempered by the guilt he felt over the way he'd treated Sara—especially after the excellent detective work she'd done on the bribed caddie. And of course, hanging over him every minute were his worries about postponing the hearing. But there was nothing he could do about that now, short of dropping out of the tournament. And *that*, he couldn't do.

He picked up his car phone and punched in the number the caddiemaster at Spyglass had given him.

"Hullo?"

Kevin hung up, wondering if maybe his luck was changing. Willie was going to loop for him tomorrow, and the little turd from Spyglass was home. Now if only Sara was home, too. He needed her to help him with Bruce tonight. If that meant telling her the truth about why he was playing in the tournament, well then, that's what he'd have to do. Sharing his burden with someone just might lighten it a little. He punched in her number and she answered after three rings.

"Sara, it's Kevin."

"Hello, Mr. Courtney." Her voice was frosty, to say the least.

"I don't blame you for being angry."

"I'll sleep much better knowing that, Mr. Courtney."

"Sara, I need your help tonight."

"Oh, didn't I tell you? My office hours are 8:30 to 5:00."

"C'mon, Sara, get over it."

"What, get over being rudely treated like I was one of your employees? How would you suggest I do that?"

"By accepting my apology," Kevin said. "I was completely out of line and I'm sorry."

There was no response.

"Look, I know why my caddie was paid off," Kevin said, "and I think I know who's behind it. But I need you to help me pin it down."

"How?"

"We'll convince Bruce to tell the truth. You being an attorney should give him something to think about."

"I hope you're not talking about strong-arm stuff."

"No. Just a little friendly persuasion."

Sara was quiet for about 30 seconds. Then he heard her sigh. "Okay, I'll help you."

"Thanks. I'll pick you up at your place in about 15 minutes."

The clock in Kevin's car read 8:30 p.m. when Sara opened the passenger-side door and got in. She was wearing jeans, a white pullover sweater and a yellow jacket trimmed in navy.

"Before we start out on this clandestine expedition," she said, locking her seatbelt into place, "you should know the firm will expect me to charge you for my time."

"Of course," Kevin replied.

"You sure I don't need my brass knuckles?"

"Nope. Just that belligerent tone you were using a little while ago."

"Scare the hell out of the kid, in other words."

"Yeah."

"No problem," Sara said.

As the Riviera headed toward Bruce's, Kevin told her about the meeting with Komoto and the bet and the pledge of secrecy. "That's why I got so touchy when you suggested that I might be hiding something."

"But now you've decided it's worth violating that pledge if I help you with Bruce."

He looked at her. "Maybe the lawyer-client relationship means I'm not violating it."

"Very possible. I only wish that brilliant revelation had emerged from your brain a few days ago."

Kevin shrugged. "I wanted to tell you about the agreement this afternoon, when you said I didn't want Joey as much as you thought."

"How good is this Noro guy?"

"Ranked number one in the world."

Sara let out a low whistle. "I'd say you didn't need those two penalty strokes."

"My flaky amateur partner cost me a stroke or two as well."

"Take away those four strokes, Kevin, and you and that guy are tied."

"Yup."

"Question. If you're that good, why are you here and not playing full time?"

"I didn't always handle the pressure very well. Some players thrive on the pressure; others find it difficult to deal with. Fear of failure, maybe."

"What, there won't be any pressure this week?"

"The way I kept it together at Spyglass today gave me some confidence. I'm hoping it carries over the next three rounds."

"Another question."

Kevin nodded.

"If Bruce *does* spill everything, how will that help you?"

"I, uh, shit, I don't know. That's your department. Isn't it illegal?"

"Probably. But there's no way we could prove anything by Sunday. Or maybe even ever. A caddie's word against Komoto's? Komoto wins every time."

Kevin's shoulders sagged.

"What about that penalty, though?" Sara asked. "If Bruce told the officials what he did, wouldn't they rescind it?"

"It's too late. I've already signed my scorecard. Besides, if word of a conspiracy gets out—and the reason for it—the news media will descend on Pebble Beach like the plague."

"Do you have the agreement that you signed?"

Kevin took the folded piece of paper out of the car's console, handed it to Sara and waited while she read it. "Is it legal?"

"Crude, but probably adequate."

He let up on the accelerator. "Well then, why should we bother to talk to Bruce if it won't do any good?"

Sara shrugged. "We've come this far, we might as well see how it plays out."

After they located Bruce's house and parked the car, they climbed two sagging wooden steps onto a darkened porch. Kevin knocked on the door. Moments later, a light came on and the door opened. Bruce was wearing dark jeans, a gray sweatshirt, and a startled expression.

"May we come in?" Kevin asked. "This lady is an attorney."

The boy quickly tried to shut the door but Kevin blocked it with his foot.

"Accepting a bribe is a felony," Sara said. "If you answer a few questions, you may not have to go to jail."

"What kind of questions?"

"How about we explain inside," Kevin said.

"I'm the only one home."

Kevin eased the door open and Sara followed him past Bruce and into the living room.

"You can't come in here threatening me," Bruce said.

"We aren't threatening you, merely stating a fact," Sara said. "Shall we sit or do you want to stand?"

Shrugging his shoulders, the caddie remained standing.

"Look, Bruce," Sara said, "I saw you accept an envelope in the parking lot after Mr. Courtney's round this afternoon. How much money were you paid to have that penalty called on him?"

"I don't know what you're talking about," Bruce sneered. "Nobody paid me nothing." He looked at Kevin. "Especially this joker here. Forty bucks for 18 holes? Boy, are you cheap."

"You're lucky you got *that* much," Kevin said.

"Listen, son," Sara said, getting his attention again, "if you force us to prove what I saw in the parking lot today, you'll have to hire an attorney, go to court, and very possibly go to jail if you're convicted. Think you'd like that? Think your parents would like throwing away their hard-earned money on an attorney?"

Bruce looked down at his feet. "It's only my mom," he said.

"Well, you think *she'd* like it? Lawyers like me cost a lot of money. A *lot* of money."

The kid looked up at her. "You promise you won't do nothing to me?"

"Yes, if you tell us the truth."

Tiny beads of sweat appeared on his forehead. He twisted his mouth around and bit on his lip.

"Who gave you the envelope," Sara asked.

"I don't know who it was; I didn't see his face. He had on a jacket with a hood and I never saw inside. Even had a glove on his hand."

"Are you sure it was a man?"

Bruce looked at her, as if it had never even occurred to him that it was anything but. "No."

"Anything special about the jacket?"

"Uh-uh."

"This person say anything to you?"

"No, but..." He hesitated.

"What?"

"The car smelled like perfume."

Kevin stared at him. "Perfume?"

"The car or the person?" Sara asked.

Bruce shrugged. "Couldn't tell."

"Could it've been men's aftershave?" Sara said.

"Smelled like perfume."

"How was this all set up, Bruce?" Sara asked.

"I got a phone call Tuesday night."

"Man or woman?"

"Couldn't tell, the voice was all garbly."

"What did the voice say?"

"I was told to do something to make a penalty."

"Did you know what to do or did the person tell you what to do?"

"They said a couple things and I picked one." He glanced at Kevin then looked away.

"If Mr. Courtney hadn't fired you, were you supposed to do something tomorrow, too?"

"Didn't say anything about tomorrow. I was pretty sure I'd get fired for it."

"How much were you paid?"

He looked away and began biting his lower lip again.

"How much, son?"

"Thousand dollars."

"Where's the money?"

He glanced quickly toward a door at the end of a hallway then looked back. "I put it in the bank," he said.

Sara sighed. "Unless you want to take a chance on going to jail, Bruce, I suggest you go down that hall to your bedroom and get the money."

The kid didn't move.

"Ever hear of the word 'evidence,' Bruce?" Sara asked.

He nodded.

"Well, that money is evidence in a crime, son. And your fingerprints are all over it."

When Kevin saw him swallow, he knew they had him.

Three minutes later, they were sitting in the Riviera staring at an envelope that contained 10 one-hundred-dollar bills. Kevin started the car and pulled away from the curb. "So tell me," he said. "What all did we learn?"

"That somebody *in addition* to Noro is trying to keep you from beating him," Sara said. "Could be Komoto, could be somebody else. Could be Komoto *and* somebody else."

"You'll keep the money as evidence?"

"It's really not evidence yet, but yeah, I'll hang onto it. If it turns out we can't prove anything, I'll figure out what to do with it then."

Kevin heaved a sigh of resignation. "You were right, Sara. Even if Bruce had said that it was Komoto who hired him, I don't know what we would've done about it."

"Which means," Sara said, "that until we get something more substantial, I'm afraid you're going to have to beat that Noro person."

"Yeah, I know. But at least I'll have some help." He told her all about Willie.

"Wow, you've had quite a day," Sara said. "When did you last eat?"

"This morning."

"I have some leftover stir-fry at home, if you're interested."

"I wouldn't want to impose."

Sara burst out laughing. "What do you call dragging me over to that kid's house? C'mon, let's go to my place and get something to eat. And tonight's *pro bono*, okay? A freebie."

"Yeah, why?"

"Maybe it's those two strokes," she said. "You've paid enough today."

The first thing Sara did when they got to her house was to light a fire in the fireplace. She got drinks next, then went back into the kitchen to heat up the food. When it was ready, Kevin ate like he'd been starving. Sara watched him in silence with a small smile on her face.

He was surprised that he felt so comfortable. Was it because of her, *specifically*, or because he really hadn't relaxed in about three days? In any case, Sara's clock on the mantel told him he couldn't relax long; it'd been 17 hours since he'd gotten out of bed that morning. He had things to do early the next morning at the pro shop, then would meet Willie on the range at 10:15. He needed to get to bed.

"Kevin, may I make a suggestion?"

"Sure."

"Something we were taught in law school might be applicable to your playing."

"Such as?"

"One of our courses in trial law dealt with psychology," Sara began.

"I was a psych major at Stanford."

"Then forgive me if you already know about this. Anyhow, we spent a lot of time on how to handle pressure. When you feel pressure during a tournament, do you tell yourself to relax?"

"Sure."

"We were taught that by doing so, it actually *increases* the tension. Besides the pressure of trying to play well, now you have the added pressure of trying *not* to be tight."

"Run that by me again, please," Kevin said.

After she had repeated it, he was thoughtful for several seconds. "Are you saying that I should leave my mind alone?"

"Exactly."

"Kind of interesting. Go on."

"That's it, basically. What it does is allow you to focus on your game, rather than on yourself and your feelings."

"Sounds too simple."

"It is simple. That's the beauty of it."

"Looks like I have two things to thank you for. No, wait. Counting you're going with me to see Bruce, that's three."

"You're welcome. Now, if you don't mind a little business, there's one point we didn't discuss the other night."

Kevin tensed. "What?"

"Does your ex-wife love Joey?"

"I suppose so."

"Does he love *her*?"

"Yes, of course."

"Do you want him to?"

"Of course, I want him to love his mother," Kevin replied. "Why are you asking me these things?"

"Because I'm your attorney, and I'm trying to get a handle on the situation."

"I see. Well, if you're wondering whether I want Joey to love me more than his mother, the answer is 'no.' What I want is to be able to be as good a father as I can, and I don't feel I can do that if I don't see him very often."

"With all your responsibilities as head pro at one of the busiest and most famous golf courses in the world," Sara said, "how do you expect to find this extra time?"

Kevin stared at her, puzzled by the tone of the questions. "What's up with this?" he asked finally. "I'll find the time, all right?" He stood up and took his dishes into the kitchen, then went straight to the front door and opened it.

Sara said, "Listen, I didn't mean..."

"Thanks again for your help tonight," Kevin said, cutting her off. "I have to get home and get some sleep."

"I'm on your side, Kevin."

Just before he closed the door behind him, Kevin said, "*That* sure makes me feel good."

CHAPTER 5

Although the tournament was now burdened with the cumbersome title of "AT&T Pebble Beach National Pro-Am," for many people it would always be known simply and reverently as "The Crosby." It began in 1937 when entertainer Bing Crosby, wanting to share with his fellow-members of the Lakewood Country Club the pleasure of both playing and socializing with professional golfers, organized a little tournament at the Rancho Santa Fe golf course near his ranch in San Diego County. The tournament was discontinued during World War II; by the time the war ended, the crooner had disposed of his San Diego interests. He was then a member of the Cypress Point Club on the Monterey Peninsula, the spectacularly beautiful 33-square-mile piece of real estate with two famous golf courses, Cypress Point and Pebble Beach, and he decided to resume the tournament there.

Entertainment celebrities—marquee legends such as Bob Hope, Phil Harris, Dean Martin, James Garner, Clint Eastwood, Andy Williams, Tennessee Ernie Ford, and Jack Lemmon—

are synonymous with The Crosby, as are famous athletes from other sports. For countless years, television viewers agonized with Lemmon as he and his various professional partners struggled to qualify and play on the tournament's final day. It was always in vain. Yet, in an exercise of masochism which only a golfer could understand, Lemmon (who said he would rather play *Hamlet* on Broadway without a rehearsal than tee it up in front of the gallery packed around the first hole) and other high-handicap amateurs would return again and again to subject themselves to the scrutiny of the spectators. And to the capricious wrath of winter weather on the Peninsula.

At seven o'clock Friday morning, Sally Kendal poured black coffee into a mug sitting on the restaurant counter in front of Kevin. He took several sips of the hot liquid, a miracle drug that erased cobwebs and activated both mind and body.

"You think I should turn you in, Kevin?"

He stared at her. "What?"

"Turn you in, for the reward."

"Whatever you're on, Sally, you better cut down the dosage."

She thrust a newspaper in front of him. "After what you did yesterday, you surely have to be on the 'Most Wanted' list."

The paper was turned to the sports section. A picture of Dean Adams headed his column at the top of the page.

Courtney Conduct
Childish, Cruel
Kevin Courtney, golf honcho at Pebble Beach and one-time tour player came out of retirement yesterday. It turned out to be a black day for his caddie, his amateur partner, and the AT&T Pebble Beach National Pro-Am.

Okay, his caddie did a boo-boo and cost Courtney a

penalty. So he fired the kid. I mean, it's not like Courtney is going to win the tournament. This is a team event, his amateur partner birdied the hole, everyone should be happy. But there is one kid who definitely isn't jumping for joy. Without a job on the biggest weekend of the year, he must be disillusioned about mankind.

Courtney was just warming up, though. On the 17th green he accused his partner of cheating. Then, after hitting a terrible drive on 18, our local hero got in his partner's face and said the bad drive was his fault. The shaken partner walked in.

I don't blame him, do you? He came here to play golf with a professional and to have a good time, not knowing that this would require being insulted by someone who...

I don't have to read this crap, Kevin thought. He resisted the temptation to wad up the newspaper. Instead he put it on the counter, took a sip of coffee, and waited for Sally to return from the kitchen.

"From the picture of that weirdo," she said, "it's what I'd expect. That article isn't the Kevin I know."

"Didn't you raise your daughter by yourself?"

"You got that right. My ex bailed out before she was one." Sally eyed him suspiciously. "What's that got to do with Weirdo?"

"Nothing. How much harder was it raising her alone than working here?"

"About a trillion times."

Thankfully, other customers came in and Sally got busy with them. Kevin ate his bacon and eggs in silence, then left a two-dollar tip. His assistants at the pro shop were furious about the column; he was the one who had to calm *them.*

It would be another hour before Kevin's name was announced

on the first tee. He would be playing the course where he worked. Since only the action at Pebble Beach would be televised on Saturday, the schedulers arranged for celebrity amateurs and golf's top money winners to cavort in front of the cameras on that day. The Courtney-Caldwell team, now perhaps minus one member—Kevin hadn't heard a word from Larry—failed to meet either of these criteria, so would perform at Pebble today and in the relative obscurity of Cypress Point the next day.

Noro was playing at Spyglass Hill. His 68 yesterday at Cypress was impressive. It was only one shot off the lead held by a player Kevin knew little about and really didn't care about. Noro was the one he had to beat.

As the Oldsmobile courtesy car shuttled him from the golf course to the practice range, Kevin thought of the folded piece of paper in the console of his car. It said he had to beat Noro; even a tie wouldn't save Pebble Beach. He was annoyed with himself for not having it worded that Noro had to beat him. Komoto was so confident he probably would have agreed to it.

Kevin's eyes strained for a glimpse of his new caddie. Willie was supposed to meet him at 10:15. Why hadn't he arranged for someone to pick up the old Scotsman at his house? What if Willie didn't show?

To Kevin's relief, Willie was waiting for him when he arrived at the range. He was wearing a blue tam but it wasn't big enough to hide all the sprouts of white hair. His plaid mackinaw was appropriate for the raw wind whipping in from Carmel Bay. It was typical "Crosby weather," with the elements promising a challenge equal to that provided by the golf course.

Famed columnist Jim Murray once observed, "The wind turns your ears purple. The cold makes your nose run and your eyes watery. The rain makes a swamp of the fairway." Yet, each year hundreds of golfers try to beg—or bribe—their way into the event. A stranger once approached the tournament chairman in a restroom at the Los Angeles airport and said, "I have $25,000 dollars in my pocket, and it's yours if I get in the Crosby."

He didn't get in.

"Glad to see you, Willie," Kevin said as he climbed out of the courtesy car.

"Aye, lad, the same goes for me."

Over Willie's shoulder, Kevin spotted Larry Caldwell walking toward them, once again resembling a peacock. The cocky, arrogant smile was gone, though. His brown eyes held Kevin's for an instant, then lowered before seeking contact again. Tentatively, he extended his hand.

"I apologize for fucking up, Kev. I promise it won't happen today. Word of honor."

Dressed conservatively in tan slacks, white shirt, and navy blue windbreaker, Kevin hesitated only momentarily before shaking his partner's hand. "Yesterday never happened as far as I'm concerned, Larry. This is the world's greatest golf course. Let's enjoy it."

Larry gave Kevin's hand an extra squeeze. "You got that right, partner. I'll enjoy it a hell of a lot more if we win this mother."

Kevin turned back to Willie and accepted a brand-new glove that his caddie had taken from the bag. Kevin worked his left hand into it, did a few stretching exercises, then pulled the sand wedge from his bag and began hitting soft, 60-yard shots.

Using a damp towel, Willie carefully cleaned each club after Kevin finished with it. The rest of the time, Kevin knew, his caddie was intently watching his swing and the flight of the ball.

"We'll do well, lad," Willie said after Kevin completed his 30-minute warm-up, "we'll do well."

It was more encouragement than he'd gotten from Bruce in five hours. Kevin winked at Willie and nodded in agreement.

"With a swing as smooth as that, my boy, you should still be playing the Tour."

"Maybe I didn't have the right caddie." He patted Willie's shoulder. "I'm glad you're along."

"This is where I belong, not in that house feeling sorry for myself."

Willie rode with Kevin in the courtesy car on the way back to the practice green. After a few minutes of putting, it was time to report to the first tee. Kevin never liked to get there too early; it gave the butterflies time to assemble in his stomach, and the gremlins in his brain.

He shook hands with the starter and was handed the scorecard for Lou Jackson and his amateur partner. He was ready to tee it up but was stopped because someone in the group ahead had lost a ball in some bushes.

The last thing Kevin needed to think about was errant teeshots and penalty strokes. He took the headcover off his driver and held the club up for Willie's inspection. "What do you think of these titanium things?"

"I gather they do the job, lad; more and more golfers seem to have one."

"This thing gives me 10 to 15 more yards, without sacrificing accuracy. If anything, my control is *better*."

Less than enthusiastically, Willie said, "I'm sure it 'tis."

Kevin knew what the old Scotsman was thinking. "You miss the sound of persimmon meeting balata, don't you?"

Willie nodded.

"I do, too," Kevin admitted. He stuck the driver back in his bag.

There were five times as many spectators around the first tee as there were at Spyglass the day before. Pebble always attracted the majority of the crowd. In a loud voice, the starter said, "Please welcome Kevin Courtney, the host professional here at Pebble Beach."

Kevin nodded and touched the bill of his visor in acknowledgment of the spirited applause. When he also heard a few boos, his annoyance at Dean Adams's column in the newspaper that morning reemerged.

Since Kevin knew that his titanium driver could power a tee-shot through the fairway of the 373-yard dogleg right, he had chosen to hit a 3-wood. Ninety percent of his concentration was focused on making a smooth swing. Sometimes, however, 90 percent isn't enough. Today it wasn't. The ball ballooned right and came down near the trees and bushes the player in the group ahead had been in.

Kevin was lucky to have a clear shot to the green, but the deep rough turned his 9-iron approach and caused the ball to go left of the green. He chipped to within six feet of the flag, but didn't come close to holing the par putt. Willie waited for the others to finish. "Your tempo was perfect on the practice tee." He held up his right index finger and moved it back and forth. "The same every time. Just like a metronome."

No way could Bruce have understood about tempo. All he knew was that he was going to make a thousand dollars. Kevin nodded gratefully at Willie. He visualized a metronome while waiting to tee off on two, then watched his drive carry 265 yards and roll an additional 20. His 2-iron on the par-5 hole stopped 10 feet from the flagstick. After knocking the eagle putt into the center of the cup, Kevin got a pat on the back from his caddie.

The bogey-eagle start took care of the stroke that Larry had cost him in the first round. Now he had to get back Bruce's two penalty strokes. On the third hole, after a perfect drive cut off much of the dogleg and should have left an easy wedge, Kevin found the ball in a divot and had to work to salvage a par. He birdied four, only to give it back on five when his 6-iron hit a rake in the bunker and caromed 60 feet away. Still annoyed at the bad break, he failed to birdie the par-5 sixth.

Willie continued to nod encouragement while Kevin continued to swing well. Yet a par on seven left him only one under—and the heart of Pebble Beach still lay ahead. Disappointed and frustrated, he stood on the tee of the 431-yard eighth hole, wondering if Willie's metronome or anything else could enable him to shoot his target score of 4-under 68.

Mother Goose was working well. But would it be enough when he was facing the most challenging three-quarters of a mile in all of golf? In the 1965 Crosby, defending champion Tony Lema told his amateur partner, "You'll have to get bogeys on these next three holes and with your strokes we'll get out alive. There's no way I can par them all."

Kevin realized that he was getting ahead of himself. *Leave your mind alone*, he thought, *like Sara said*. Thankfully, the wind had abated to only a breeze and the sun was peeking out from behind the clouds. Taking off his blue windbreaker, Kevin looked up the hill that hid the landing area of what

Arnold Palmer called "the best par-4 hole I've ever played." The blind tee shot to a flat clifftop plateau gives no inkling of the spectacular right-angle second shot across a gaping oceanic chasm.

A 3-wood or 1-iron? He put his hand on the iron and glanced at Willie for confirmation. The Scotsman nodded, slowly moving his index finger back and forth.

A confident swing sent the ball over the hill and onto the plateau of the fairway. Jack Nicklaus described the approach at Pebble's eighth as his favorite shot in all golf. Kevin was 187 yards away, and between him and the green was a chasm that dropped a hundred feet into Carmel Bay. In one Crosby, Johnny Miller drove to within six precarious inches of the precipice and said when he hit his second shot that it was the hardest his heart had ever beat in his life. But usually it was intimidating only to amateurs who annually deposit 30,000 balls into the bay. Professionals are challenged more by the task of hitting the tiny green perched on the opposite bank and surrounded by five large bunkers.

"What do you think?" Kevin asked Willie, pulling out a 5-iron. With the wind blowing from right to left—and twice as strong because they were up on the plateau—if Kevin hit his normal draw, he would have to start the ball out over the ocean and the cliff to the right of the green. "Maybe I should try to cut it in from the left."

"Are you sure of that shot, lad?"

"Not a hundred percent, but I think I can pull it off."

"Myself, I like a punched 4-iron the wind can't play with so much," Willie said.

"Yeah, but I may be able to get this closer."

"If you hit it perfectly," Willie said gently. "Otherwise, you could be burdened with a high number."

Kevin didn't want any more burdens. He stared at the green and the trouble flanking it on both sides before tossing up several blades of grass and watching them blow almost horizontally. He took out the longer iron and hit it crisply toward the right edge of the green.

"Leave it alone, wind!" Kevin begged as the ball was blown toward a left bunker. But it caught the edge of the green, stopping some 20 feet above the hole.

"Good call," he murmured to Willie.

"That's what I'm here for, lad."

Unwilling to charge the putt and risk leaving a six-footer coming back, Kevin lagged the ball and watched without breathing as it rolled and rolled and rolled and then gloriously disappeared into the cup.

He reined in his emotions and looked toward the ninth hole, one of the most difficult par-4s in golf. It extends 464 yards along the top of the bluff high above the Pacific. The downhill fairway slopes toward the ocean. His draw was made for this hole; it would prevent the ball from running down the slope and over the cliff. He drove it perfectly, followed up with a 6-iron to the center of the green, and then two-putted for par.

The tenth, the last of the par-4 bluff holes, is slightly shorter—426 yards to the farthest corner of the course. The green is small, hugging the edge of the cliff. After another good drive, Kevin tried to guide his 7-iron, and the wind pushed it left of the green. A delicate sand wedge over a bunker gave him a 6-foot putt, which he holed. He had conquered the impregnable trio by playing them one under par.

Catching his breath while waiting for the others to finish

putting, Kevin looked toward the distant Carmel Beach and could see several people taking advantage of the partly sunny skies. On one of his and Joey's Saturdays last fall, they had gone there for a picnic. Joey had spread the peanut butter and jelly on their sandwiches, washed the apples, and wrapped the cookies in foil.

The water was too cold for swimming, but after lunch they waded in Carmel Bay. Then they ran on the beach, Joey teasing his dad because he wasn't keeping up, and turned around less than 50 feet from where Kevin was now standing. When they passed by an elderly couple walking along the sand, Joey pointed up toward the course and proudly said, "My dad works there."

Now it was time to go back to work. Larry had just rolled in a five-foot putt for par and a net birdie, his second of the round. There was the usual high five, but Larry wasn't as exuberant as yesterday. Kevin realized that he had been so intense about his own game that he had practically ignored his partner.

"Great par," he said, patting Larry on the shoulder as they walked off the green. "That's one of the hardest holes out here."

Larry's grin couldn't have been broader if he'd been told he played the hole like Nicklaus.

Kaori Noro had an early starting time at Spyglass Hill. What if he shot another 68, Kevin wondered, or even lower? He had avoided looking at the leader boards up to that point. But on the 11th tee, while waiting for the foursome ahead to play their second shots, he took a look. Noro's name was fourth from the top. He'd had a 71 at Spyglass—an average round—and it put him only three strokes ahead of Kevin.

Kevin's play over the last three holes had given him new

confidence, and, he felt, there was no reason he couldn't make up at least two of those strokes on the last eight holes. For the first time he felt he actually had a chance of winning, of saving Pebble Beach. He wondered if Noro knew about the agreement. If he did, was it putting additional pressure on him? It couldn't be as much as the pressure on Kevin. *Leave your mind alone.* Kevin turned away from the leader board.

The 11th hole plays inland toward the forest. It's a relatively short par-4 of 384 yards, with out-of-bounds on the right. A good drive should leave no more than a pitching wedge to the long narrow green and a legitimate chance for birdie. Kevin played the hole perfectly, but a spike mark on the green deflected his relatively short putt and the result was a disappointing par.

Those things happen; shake it off.

Standing on the 12th tee, Kevin looked at the green some 200 yards away. Lou Jackson was up first, so Kevin automatically glanced in his fellow pro's bag to see what club he used. When it was his turn, he chose a 3-iron, took a practice swing, reminded himself to leave his mind alone, and breathed a "Thank You" to Sara when the Titleist found the putting surface some 30 feet from the hole. He was happy to walk off the green with a par.

Larry came over and walked along with him to the next hole. "Explain something to me, will you, Kev?"

"What?"

"On the tee back there, it appeared to me that you looked in Lou's bag to see what club he used. Right?"

"Right."

"That's not cheating?"

Kevin suddenly wondered if Larry was about to make

another scene, or whether he was simply curious.

Larry kept pace. "I mean, I accidentally touch a few grains of sand and you call a penalty on me. *You* look in the other guy's bag and it's okay. Right?"

"What you did is against the rules, Larry," Kevin said. "What I did, isn't. Every pro looks."

"Ah. Well, kind of sounds like a double standard to me."

Kevin stopped in his tracks, but Larry kept walking toward the tee. Over his shoulder, Larry said, "Nice par back there, partner."

Double standard, Kevin thought. *Much like me saying that I want to spend more time with my son...but apparently— hell, clearly—I want to save a golf course more.* Walking on toward the tee, Kevin wondered if Sara *and* Larry were right. Maybe he *was* a jerk.

Since Lou Jackson had bogeyed 12, Kevin had the honor. Thirteen is a 392-yard par-4, with a treacherous green demanding an approach that kept the ball below the hole. On the previous tee, Kevin had been able to leave his mind alone. But now, as he addressed the ball, he kept thinking about Larry's comments. Sara hadn't told him what to do when someone else was messing with his mind, nor did Mother Goose have anything to offer. He pulled his drive into a large bunker left of the fairway, hit a nice 7-iron onto the green's top shelf, but then carelessly three-putted. He was now four strokes behind Noro.

As they walked onto 14 tee, Kevin murmured to Willie, "This'll be a metronome swing if I have to stand here all day to get my composure."

"Aye, lad, patience."

He did hit a good drive on the dogleg right par-5. The

hole's length made it unreachable in two, so he hit a perfect layup that left him 95 yards from the green. His third shot with a sand wedge landed on the top level where the flagstick was located, but the ball spun backward, caught the steep face in the middle, and rolled all the way to the front of the green. It was an impossible 50-foot putt. But somehow—miraculously—Kevin made it. The crowd around the green roared when the ball dropped, and Kevin got high fives from everyone—even Larry Caldwell.

After routine pars at the next three holes, he stood on the tee of the famed 548-yard finishing hole knowing a birdie would give him a 69 and leave him only two strokes behind Noro. Larry had not made any more pars, and had not really spoken since his "double standard" comments five holes earlier.

Kevin started to pull the 3-wood from his bag, then pushed it back and reached for his 1-iron. The decision produced an affirmative nod from Willie. With Carmel Bay to the left and out-of-bounds to the right, Kevin knew that a safe play was the smart play. He widened his stance for some stability against the buffeting wind off the bay, then wasted little time drawing the club back. Coming down again a micro-second later, he caught the ball solidly and sent it on its way. When the ball finally came to a stop, it was in the center of the fairway and 235 yards closer to the green.

The shot was rewarded by cheers from the gallery, which had grown to several hundred as word spread that the host pro was fashioning a superb round at Pebble Beach. Several long, deep breaths helped to relax him as he walked to the ball. He then chose to lay up with a 5-iron, and that left him with about 110 yards to the green. His third shot, with a pitching wedge, was greeted by a huge roar when it nearly flew into the hole. "Lovely," Willie told him.

Standing over the five-foot putt, Kevin worried about the ball moving in the wind. Taking no extra time, he stroked the ball into the center of the cup.

Kevin nodded in acknowledgment of the gallery's enthusiastic response, then shook hands with the other two players in the group and their caddies. He looked around for his partner but only caught a glimpse of Larry's back as he pulled another disappearing act. Kevin was disappointed. Sitting at 13 under par for the two rounds, the team had a good chance of improving their score on Saturday and making the cut. Most amateurs in Larry's situation would be celebrating. It was too bad his childishness wouldn't allow him to enjoy the moment.

After verifying his 69, and signing his card, Kevin left the scorer's tent and checked the nearby leader board. For the first time during the tournament, his name was on it. Noro was currently in second place, and Kevin was two strokes back. The man he had to beat—the best player in the world—was still in sight.

One of the Tour officials interrupted Kevin's thoughts. "Good playing out there," he said, smiling. "And everybody in the media center would like to hear all about it."

CHAPTER 6

"What did you do to your amateur partner *this* time?"

When a player is invited to visit with the media, he or she is usually expected to give a brief overview of the round—birdies, bogeys, clubs used on various shots, good or bad breaks, what he thinks of the golf course, etc. The floor is then open to the reporters and writers to ask questions. But Kevin was hardly seated beside Richard Gardner in the media room when Dean Adams started badgering him.

"We partnered well," Kevin replied. He turned his head and looked at Gardner. "What are we, only four or five strokes out of the team lead?"

Dean Adams didn't give the Director of Communications time to answer. "Then why did he leave without shaking hands, or even waiting for you to putt out on 18?"

Kevin stared at the newspaper columnist. "That weirdo," as Sally the waitress had referred to him that morning, was wearing jeans and a grubby-looking sweatshirt. "I'm afraid you'll have to ask *him*," Kevin said. "I don't know."

"How did you feel when you drove it in the trees on Number One?" someone asked.

Kevin grinned before he answered. "Like I was the 'Am' part of the team instead of the 'Pro' part." It got a laugh. "Actually, I thought of a playing lesson that I gave last week on course management. Fortunately, I was able to get back on track with the eagle on two. The birdie on eight felt like another eagle."

"What did you hit for your second shot?"

"At eight, I couldn't decide between a solid 5 or a knock-down 4. My caddie liked the 4, so that's what I hit. Obviously, he was right."

"Who was your caddie today?"

Kevin told them about Willie and his Scottish background. "I seriously doubt that I would be 3 under without him. Today was the first time he saw me play, and he clubbed me perfectly."

"Is that why you didn't fire him?" Adams asked, "Like that poor little kid yesterday?"

"Oh I fired Willie, all right," Kevin replied, casually. "I always fire my caddie after he does a good job. Didn't you know that?"

Adams's face reddened. "Can he keep you from choking tomorrow, like you did when you were playing on the Tour full time?"

"If you mean," Kevin said, "can my caddie perform the Heimlich maneuver, the answer is 'yes.'" He smiled sweetly at Adams. "Thank you for being so concerned."

Kevin heard several people in the room chuckle, including the Director of Communications. He looked away from Adams and saw that another player was being ushered in for an interview. "That it?"

"How much golf have you played in the last six months," someone asked, "both recreational and competitive?"

"*Maybe* 10 rounds, total. Competitive? I accepted a challenge by one of the assistants a while back and he beat me by three shots."

"Then how do you account for your strong showing this week?"

"Yesterday, I was lucky. Today, it was my caddie. The moon and the tides may have had something to do with it, too. I know I can count on Willie again tomorrow; I'm not so sure about the lunar part."

When there weren't any more questions from the media, Gardner thanked Kevin for coming and wished him good luck in the next round. Kevin left the room.

On the way to the pro shop, he was stopped several times by autograph seekers. Signing his name on programs and caps brought back pleasant memories—plus a few unwelcome butterflies. The requests meant that he was getting attention, and the attention always caused more pressure.

It was nearly dark when he left the pro shop to walk out to the 18th tee. Two contestants were still working on the putting green; several couples were window-shopping the stores below the Media Center; others were entering The Lodge for dinner or drinks. Kevin pulled the collar of his dark green windbreaker tight around his neck when the cold wind off Carmel Bay hit him as he moved beyond the shelter of the buildings.

The 18th green always looked odd without a flagstick; a member of the grounds crew had removed it after the day's last foursome had finished. The tide was out, so Kevin didn't get wet from waves slapping against the seawall and the rocks that bordered the hole. It was amazing how the fresh, clean air and the spectacular scenery helped drain the tension from his neck and shoulders. Considering the pressure he knew he would be under the next day at Cypress Point, it was surprising how relaxed he felt by the time he reached the tee.

Kevin walked to the very tip, where it jutted out into Carmel Bay and where, when the tide was in and the wind was howling, it was like standing in the middle of a storm. Now only the cold air washed over him as he turned back to face the fairway. When he arrived at this hole on Sunday, would he still have a chance to beat Noro? Or would the bet have been decided long before? Would he play like a Touring Pro tomorrow, or like the club pro he now was?

Through the near darkness, off to his right, Kevin saw a figure approaching. "I'm sorry," he called, "but the golf course is closed."

"Kevin?"

He smiled when he recognized Sara's voice. "What the hell are you doing out here?"

"Freezing my butt off, if you want to know the truth."

He could now see that she was wearing slacks, a short-sleeved shirt and a sweater vest as her only protection against a February evening on the Peninsula. What Kevin guessed was a Coach leather purse was slung over her right shoulder.

"Where's your jacket, for God's sake?"

"I didn't bring one," Sara said. "Thought I'd find you in the pro shop, not halfway to Carmel."

When she arrived at where he was standing, Kevin suddenly realized how glad he was to see her. "Here," he said, unzipping his windbreaker.

"That's okay, I'm fine."

"Don't be so stubborn for once," Kevin said. She sighed,

but accepted the jacket and put it on. "So, counselor, what are you doing out here?"

"The question is, what're *you* doing out here?"

Kevin smiled again, something he'd noticed he hadn't done much of lately. "It's kind of a daily ritual," he said. "Helps me wind down. I do some serious thinking out here sometimes. Other times, I try not to think about anything."

"Which were you doing when I intruded?"

He shrugged his shoulders. "Can't remember. But I do know I'm ready to go back."

After a few steps, Sara said, "Because I showed up?"

"No, of course not. But why *did* you show up?"

"Mostly out of duty, I'm afraid."

"That damned hearing again," he muttered.

She took his arm. "Like I said last night, Kevin, I'm on your side, so don't get upset, okay?"

He sighed.

"For a reason I can't begin to understand," Sara said, "Judge Higgins is now willing to hold your hearing *tomorrow*."

Kevin stopped. "You've got to be kidding." The moon had slipped out from behind a cloud, providing enough illumination for Kevin to clearly see Sara's face. There was no levity in it. "I didn't know the courts were open on Saturdays."

"Hey, a judge can hold a hearing whenever and wherever he wants to—in a gymnasium at midnight if that suits his fancy."

"Tomorrow could not be further from *my* fancy."

"I know. But as your attorney, it's my duty to inform you of the proposed hearing."

"Why tomorrow?" Kevin asked. "I thought his schedule was filled. If it's not, then why not on Monday? It's like he's deliberately picking times when I can't be there."

"It does seem like that, doesn't it? Maybe your ex-wife's attorney has an in with him."

"Knowing Joan," Kevin replied, "I wouldn't be surprised. If you've got your phone, you might as well tell that judge not to look for me."

"This late, all I'll get is an answering machine," Sara said. She reached inside her purse and brought out the small phone. "For my own protection, though, I had to clear it with you first."

As they resumed walking, Sara called and left an apologetic message about their not being able to make the Saturday hearing. When she was finished, Kevin said, "Thank you for being understanding about the situation."

"You're welcome." She linked her arm through his. "Now, what's this I hear about some club pro shooting 69 at Pebble Beach today."

"Pretty amazing, huh?"

"Noro's only two ahead now, right?"

"Yep."

"Damn, Kevin," she said, "without those penalty strokes yesterday..."

"I know."

Both were silent until they neared The Lodge.

"Sorry about giving you the third degree last night, Kevin," Sara said finally. "It was pretty rude."

"You were just doing your job. I should've handled it better."

"Think we could try it again tonight?"

He glanced down at her. "Try what?"

"Dinner, minus the attorney talk."

"That wasn't nearly as bad as my walking out in a huff,"

Kevin said. "Talk about rude!"

Sara thought for a few seconds. "You're right. That *was* worse." Then she smiled. "So why don't we do it right this time?"

They had reached the locked pro shop.

"Time's up, Bud," Sara said.

"I'd love to," Kevin said quickly, laughing.

"Good."

She was looking up into his face. The wind had blown a few strands of her black hair out of place, and he pushed them back. "I have two rounds left," he said, "so I really can't stay too long. Us old club pros need our rest."

"No problem." She looked at her watch. "It's 6:00. My place in an hour?"

It would give him just enough time to go home and shower. "Perfect," he said. Before she left, Sara told him he didn't need to bring anything.

On his way home, Kevin came to the conclusion that he had to take *something* to Sara's. She was going out of her way for the second night in a row, and he had to somehow thank her. He decided to bring an expensive bottle of Merlot that he had at the condo, a gift from one of his students.

The hot shower felt great, so he stayed under it as long as he could. After drying off, he put on a pair of jeans, a green and gray long-sleeved Rugby shirt with a white collar, white socks, and silver and black Nike running shoes.

It was almost seven when he walked out to the carport. In his left hand, held by the neck, was the bottle of wine; in his right, were his car keys and the door lock remote. Pushing a button on the remote, he heard the locks inside the Riviera being activated. At the same time, Kevin noticed that the carport light was out and it made him stop. He looked around slowly but neither saw nor heard anything out of the ordinary. He shook his head—suddenly feeling foolish—continued on to the car, and reached awkwardly for the door handle with his right hand.

In the dark, Kevin couldn't see what caused the searing pain in his thumb. He cried out instantly, juggled but held onto the bottle of wine, and knew simultaneously that the skin had been badly cut. He set the bottle down and tried to cover the cut with his left hand. Frightened by the blood oozing between his fingers, he ran back to the condo.

Once inside the bathroom, he hurried to the sink, put his hand in and turned on the cold faucet. The water increased the pain immediately and he winced. A couple of minutes later, blood still flowing, Kevin applied direct pressure. When that didn't help, he realized it would have to be stitched. He wrapped a bath towel around his hand, grabbed another one off the rack, and ran out of the condo to his car.

A razor blade was inserted into one side of the door handle. Using a towel to pull it out, he then opened the door and got in. By the time he turned onto W.R. Holman Highway 10 minutes later, the flowing blood had forced him to rewrap his hand. Even worse, he was feeling faint. Kevin breathed a sigh of relief when the brightly-lit sign of the Community Hospital of the Monterey Peninsula finally came into view. He pulled into the Emergency entrance, parked as close as he could to the automatic double doors, and walked inside. Twenty minutes later, after verbally providing his personal information, he was ushered by a nurse into a small room. He sat on the edge of an examining table as she began to unwrap the towel from his hand.

"So how'd this happen?"

"Cut it with a razor blade."

The nurse looked up at him over her half-glasses, as if she was about to admonish him. But she didn't. She inspected the cut, which was on the inside near the base of his right thumb. The bleeding had slowed. "It's a beauty, all right," the nurse said. Kevin closed his eyes.

"Want to lie down?"

Kevin nodded gratefully. The lightheadedness was soon gone, but he kept his eyes closed and occasionally bit his lip as the wound was cleaned.

"Mr. Courtney, I'm Dr. Glouster."

Opening his eyes, Kevin saw the smiling face of a man who appeared too young to be a doctor.

"Hello."

"How are you feeling, Mr. Courtney?"

"Better, thanks."

"I'm going to tie a little tourniquet around the base of your thumb and try to stop the bleeding. Then I'll close the cut with some sutures."

Kevin nodded, closed his eyes again and pictured the swing of his friend Hal Simpson. Hal had lost his right thumb in a childhood accident but had become an exceptional golfer in spite of the disability. Kevin tried to envision making a swing without using his right thumb. Could he even *hold* a club that way? *Son of a bitch!* he thought. *How in the hell am I going to play Cypress Point tomorrow? And who in the hell is doing this?*

"It's a nice, clean slice, Mr. Courtney," Dr. Glouster said. He got up from the stool he'd been sitting on.

"Did I cut any nerves or tendons or anything like that?"

Kevin asked.

"No. You were very lucky."

"I'll have full use of my thumb?"

"You will in a few days."

Kevin raised himself up, swung his legs around and sat on the edge of the table again. "Doctor," he said, "I have to play in a golf tournament in 12 hours. How tough is that going to be?"

"You in the pro-am?"

"Yeah."

Glouster stared at him for a few seconds. "*Kevin* Courtney? You the pro at Pebble?"

"Yeah. And I *have* to play tomorrow."

"Hmm," Glouster said thoughtfully. "Well it's going to be sore, that's for sure." He put his hands in a golf grip and squeezed them together to simulate holding a club. "There's some pressure at the base of that thumb because it sits on top of the other one. I suspect you'll feel it all the way through the swing."

"How about the stitches? Will they hold for a few days?"

"Depends on how hard you swing," Glouster said. "I'll give it my best seamstress job, but if the bandage comes off I can't guarantee anything."

"What about something for the pain?"

"We'll give you some Motrin when we're done here. Or you could take Advil. Either one will help. Now, ready to get started?"

"Yeah, let's get going."

Glouster put his hands together in a golf grip again. "By the way, what did you shoot today?"

"Sixty-nine."

"Wow. You near the lead?"

"Three shots back."

"Where do you play tomorrow?"

"Cypress."

The doctor emitted a low whistle. "That'll be a test for both of our skills."

Thirty minutes later Kevin walked out of the emergency room, his thumb sutured, bandaged, and numb. The rest of his body felt as if he'd been run over by a truck. After carefully checking the driver-side door handle on his car, he popped the locks and got inside. Using wet paper towels he'd gotten from a restroom, he attempted to clean the seats and console. Doing it left-handed was difficult.

The Riviera's clock reminded him that he was almost two hours late for dinner at Sara's. Was she worried or angry? Was she still there, or had she given up by now and gone out? Reaching for the car phone with his right hand, he lifted it gingerly out of its cradle. His reward for trying was a "beep" and a readout that said the battery was low.

Kevin said "Shit" to himself, started the engine and sat there listening to it idle. His right hand tingled.

Logic told him to go home and go to bed. He was teeing off in 10 hours, and there was no telling how much sleep he'd get once the Xylocaine wore off. He knew, though, that he'd feel better if he could call and tell Sara what happened. She might be pissed at first, but Kevin was sure she'd understand. He hoped so, anyway—he needed her. He put the car in gear with his left hand and pulled out of the parking lot.

It took 15 minutes to get to her house. Careful not to bump the steering wheel, he climbed out of the Riviera and walked up to the front door. Except for a lamp that was lit behind a shaded window to his right, the house was dark. He rang the doorbell three times and listened intently for some sound from within. None came. Sighing finally, he looked down at his right thumb and gave it the finger with his left hand.

He then walked back to the car and drove home.

CHAPTER 7

To the surprise of first-time players, the tee shot on the opening hole at the Cypress Point Club must be hit over a portion of 17-Mile Drive. There are three par-5s on the front nine, two of them back-to-back. It plays to a par of 37. Par is 35 on the back nine, with the 10th hole being the last par 5 on the course. Following it are four par 4s, then the par-3 15th and 16th, followed by two more par 4s. On paper, it might look like the layout of a municipal course designed by a committee. From the championship tees, Cypress Point measures a modest 6,536 yards. Ho hum.

These 6,536 yards, however, are different. To say that this is just another golf course is to say that Michelangelo's David is just another statue. Sandy Tatum, a former president of the United States Golf Association, once labeled Cypress Point "The Sistine Chapel of Golf." It is on every list of the five greatest golf courses in the world. Bobby Jones was so taken with Cypress the first time he played it that he invited its architect, Scottish surgeon Alister MacKenzie, to help him design Augusta National, home of the Masters.

Truth be known, MacKenzie doesn't deserve all the credit for the splendor of the Cypress Point Club. The Monterey Peninsula provided him with a spectacular setting. Still, many architects would have molded the terrain—sometimes peaceful and sometimes angry—to their concept of a golf course. The Scotsman was gifted with the rare talent and good sense to observe Mother Nature's "Do Not Disturb" sign when he accommodated his masterpiece into the wooded hillsides of the Del Monte Forest and atop the spectacular cliffs bordering the Pacific Ocean.

Cathedral pines and enchantingly-twisted Monterey cypress border many of the fairways and greens. Sandy dunes characterize the middle holes. The ocean relentlessly pounds at the very foundation upon which Cypress Point lies, while sea lions bark, gulls fly overhead, and deer meander out of the forest as a reminder that this is *their* playground. In fact, wild deer and elk enjoy greater access to the golf course than do humans. Cypress Point had never hosted a major championship. The club and its members are not interested, and their annual participation in the AT&T National Pro-Am is the only time the general public is allowed to roam the grounds. Even then, only club members and their guests are allowed in the clubhouse. Bob Hope once quipped, "We had a big membership drive—and drove out 50 members." The average daily play is about 30 golfers.

Standing on the first tee at Cypress Point at 8:40 Saturday morning in the third round of the tournament, Willie gave Kevin a new Titleist 3 that he'd just taken out of its sleeve. He also gave his player a white, wooden tee. It was the first time that Kevin's caddie had had to carry his tees for him. He didn't want to take a chance on jabbing his thumb every time he reached into his right pocket, and the glove on his left hand made it awkward getting them from the other pocket. Kevin had told Willie that he had cut himself opening a package with a utility knife. Willie's only response was to say, "After he had that car accident that almost killed him, Hogan won six more majors."

The first few swings on the practice tee had been scary. They were soft wedges, with his bandaged thumb barely riding along on the grip. Kevin flinched on the first three shots, pulling his thumb off the grip before hitting the ball. He tried again, forcing himself to keep the thumb in place. Although there was some discomfort at impact, he decided it was nothing he couldn't handle. Gradually, he gained confidence in Dr. Glouster's sutures and the Motrin and in his ability to swing normally. Still, he didn't hit as many practice balls as usual.

Kevin was conscious of the thumb when he teed up the ball for his drive on the first hole, then even more aware of it during two practice swings.

Dammit, forget about the thumb. If the stitches pull out, they pull out.

He pushed up the cuffs of his navy Gore-Tex jacket, first the right sleeve and then the left. It was a nervous reaction he wasn't even aware of making. Beneath the waterproof windbreaker were a sweater and a short-sleeved shirt. He was also wearing Gore-Tex pants over his slacks. Driving to the course, he heard on the radio that the temperature was 51° and that the wind was blowing 20 miles an hour from the west, gusting up to 30. Kevin turned off the radio, not wanting to know about the temperature or the wind gusts, not wanting anything negative. He'd had enough of that yesterday.

Today, everything would be positive—including the weather report. It would be tough at Cypress Point, but it would probably be even tougher at Pebble Beach, where Noro was playing. Holes six through ten, on the bluff high above Stillwater Cove and Carmel Bay, would be buffeted unmercifully by the wind. Seventeen and eighteen would also be extremely difficult. Kevin suddenly thought about the long and dangerous par-3 16th at Cypress but quickly put it out of his mind. He would deal with it when the time came.

Now, as he stood on the first tee, all he cared about was this one drive. After that, he would simply take it one stroke at a time. He knew he would have to concentrate as hard as he ever had before, and somehow ignore the cold and the wind. It was the only way that he would have a chance to pick up a couple of strokes on Noro.

Larry Caldwell hadn't been on the practice range, nor did Kevin see him on the putting green. He couldn't imagine that he would have dropped out, though, as much as he seemed to want to win the team title. He was right; Larry appeared on the tee a few minutes before it was time for Kevin to hit.

"Decided to stay warm instead of warming up," he said to Kevin, smiling sheepishly. "All I do when I practice is groove my mistakes, anyway."

"Not a bad strategy."

"Say, partner, what happened to your thumb?"

"Cut it opening a box."

"Too bad. Can you swing okay?"

"We'll see," Kevin said.

"Listen, I know this is getting to be a broken record, Kev," Larry said, "but I want to apologize for running out on you yesterday. *Again*. I got this temper thing, but I guess I don't need to tell you that. It'll be different today, I promise. Got me a new driver, buddy. Paid 500 bucks for that sucker. Supposed to make the ball go straight." He smiled broadly. "I ever tell you about the guy at our club?"

"Uh-uh."

"Had the biggest banana ball you ever saw. Gets himself a new driver with a hook face like you wouldn't believe. No way he could slice that mother." Larry giggled. "Me and another guy, we sneak in the bag room and replace it with one that's got this wide open face. First time the guy uses it, the ball nearly came back to him. Practically a boomerang. Boy, did we laugh."

Kevin grinned. "Wish I could've seen it. Hey, let's have some fun today. Okay?"

"You bet, Kev."

Now it was time. Kevin's eyes locked onto the landing area in the valley below. A sharp wind hit the left side of his face, confirming his plan to aim 10 yards left. Another glance at the target and he initiated the swing with a slight forward press. Muscle memory kicked in, producing a swing that propelled the ball over 17-Mile Drive exactly as programmed. But instead of watching it, Kevin was looking at his hands, cocked beyond his left ear. His thumb was still in position, the bandage still white. And he hadn't flinched. Confidence flowed through him for the first time since that startling moment he'd grabbed the door handle of the Riviera. He was ready to take on Cypress Point.

At Spyglass on Thursday, Kevin had struggled to make par on the first hole; on Friday at Pebble, he'd made bogey. He was determined to begin this round properly. When his 7-iron to the first green at Cypress stopped 15 feet left of the hole, he visualized a fast start. It was his first putt that was fast, though, goosed a bit by the strong wind. It ended up five feet past the hole. Angered by the missed opportunity, Kevin failed to make the comebacker for par. The anticipated birdie became a bogey. He rammed his putter into the bag.

"When the wind is wrathful," Willie said, "patience is rewarded."

"I can't play scared," Kevin whispered angrily, his lips tightening. "That's one of the things that got me off the Tour."

"That you can't. Let's get the stroke back on the next hole."

"I'll get it, plus the birdie I just lost."

"Patience, lad. It's going to be a long day."

Playing downwind, the 551-yard second hole was reachable with two strong shots. Kevin executed both perfectly and left himself with a 30-foot putt for eagle.

"You're putting against the wind," Willie reminded him. "Smooth but firm."

Kevin concentrated on keeping his body still and on making a solid stroke. When he looked up, the ball was halfway to the hole. It tracked perfectly and dropped into the bottom of the cup. Bogey, eagle—the same start he'd had at Pebble the day before. Somehow, though, despite the cold and the wind, he needed to better yesterday's 69.

At the par-3 third, Kevin remembered Willie's thought about patience. Downwind, with the flagstick tucked behind a bunker, it would take skill and nerves and a little bit of luck to get the ball close. The round was too young for Kevin to do anything risky, so he played to the center of the green and safely two-putted for par.

The 385-yard fourth, bordered by Monterey cypress, was

one of the two remaining downwind holes on the front side. To the left, a hundred yards from the tee, several deer were grazing. Kevin watched them momentarily, then reached for his driver. He noticed that Willie was looking at him.

"One-iron is the club," his caddie said softly.

"Downwind, I should be able to get it within a hundred yards."

"Or into the trees. It still takes two strokes to reach the green, lad."

Reluctantly, Kevin took the advice. Twenty minutes later, he tapped in a short par putt. Having just witnessed Lou Jackson hit his tee-shot into the woods and then catch a tree with his second shot, Kevin's score took on a new meaning. It was a smart par, especially since he had 32 more holes to play.

The fifth, though, was a hole he felt he had to birdie. A dogleg par-5 to the left, it swooped abruptly up a hill and was only 493 yards. A thick stand of trees bordering almost the entire left side of the fairway protected it from the wind off the ocean. After flushing his drive almost 270 yards, Kevin followed with a 2-iron, which trickled onto the front of the green. Then, instead of aggressively going for the long eagle, he stroked a safe putt, which stopped inches below the cup.

Like the fifth, the par-5 sixth could sometimes be reached with two solid shots. Due to the stiff wind in his face, though, he thought better of trying it and was satisfied to get his par and go to the short seventh. Waiting for the group ahead to finish putting, Kevin saw several spectators coming from the direction of the clubhouse. Maybe a couple of dozen bundled fans were gathered around the tee by the time he hit. No one had on more clothes than Larry Caldwell, however, and it was clearly impeding his swing. He'd hacked it around badly on the last two holes and he didn't appear to be having much fun.

They were now embarking on holes that played through rugged sand dunes. There would be fewer trees as the layout took them closer to the Pacific, assuming more and more of the characteristics of a links course.

Closer to the ocean meant more wind, which was why several of the Monterey cypress trees—some silhouetted against the blue Pacific—were twisted into grotesque forms. Atlanta newspaperman O.B. Keeler, Bobby Jones's confidant and biographer, once described them as "the crystallization of the dream of an artist who had been drinking gin and sobering up on absinthe." Adding to the challenge of these middle holes were the sand dunes, thick with clumps of knee-high grass, spiny evergreen shrubs, and the dreaded ice plant.

Perhaps even more menacing, though, especially with the wind from the Pacific already buffeting them, was knowing that the 16th hole was waiting.

Kevin got a routine par on seven. Standing on the eighth tee, he was two under for the round and five under for the tournament. A dogleg right of only 363 yards, the par 4 was going into a wind that could make it play 30 yards longer. By cutting off part of the dogleg, he could shorten the hole. He looked at his caddie.

"Patience," Willie whispered.

Kevin nodded, played it conservatively and got his par. On nine, he didn't need Willie's reminder. The downwind 291-yard par 4 was reachable if he could hit his driver straight enough to avoid the tall grass, bunkers, sand dunes, and scrub. He thought he could. But then he also thought of Tom Watson. In a practice round one year, Watson drove the green. When asked if he would use driver during the tournament, he replied, "Sure, if I want to be certain of making a seven."

A 200-yard 3-iron, a short-iron approach that bounced forward and bit on the plateaued green, and a three-foot birdie putt provided the exclamation mark for Kevin's front nine. His satisfaction was tempered, however, because his right thumb had been aching for the last half-hour. He swallowed two Motrins and, for probably the hundredth time, checked the bandage for blood.

"I thought I was supposed to be a part of this team," Larry said as they left the ninth green.

Kevin's body stiffened; the last thing he needed was for Larry to be ticked about something.

"You shot 34, right?"

"Right."

Larry grinned. "Well, how can I help the damned team if you're running the table?"

"Your net par on one helped us a lot, partner."

"Yeah, but I'm struggling now. Got any more tips like the one you gave me on Thursday?"

"How about one less layer of clothing?"

Larry peeled off his jacket and tossed it to his caddie. "Hell, I'll do a 'Lady Godiva' if it'll help us win this mother."

Laughing, Kevin figured Larry probably *would* strip if there weren't any spectators. But there were. At least 200 hardy fans were standing around the 10th tee, clearly there to watch him play. His eyes scanned the crowd and he registered several familiar faces but he didn't see Sara. He was disappointed but not surprised. Kevin turned up the collar of his windbreaker and asked Willie how he was holding up. "In Scotland," he replied with a smile, "we'd call this a beautiful day for golf."

Kevin laughed, and it relaxed him. It also caused him to lose focus for a hole.

He compensated for a disappointing par on the short, vulnerable par-5 10th with an unlikely birdie on 11. He was back to four under par on one of the world's most formidable golf courses, in winds gusting up to 30 miles an hour that were producing a wind chill that had to be near or below freezing. Even more amazing, he felt free of the fear that had driven him off the Tour five years before.

Kevin played 12 almost as well as 11, his birdie putt maddeningly lipping out. Ocean sounds—waves repeatedly thundering onto rocks—replaced the howling of wind through cypress trees as he stood on the 13th tee. Some people consider it to be the truest links-style hole at Cypress Point. No trees are in sight: only mounds, native grasses two feet tall, expanses of dunes, greenside bunkers, and the elusive fairway. To reach the fairway, his drive would have to carry at least 180 yards to clear the scruffy sand up ahead.

Ordinarily, he could fly a 6-iron that far. Into the strong wind, though, it took a solid swing and his new titanium driver to barely get the job done. A rope of a 5-iron left a long putt from below the hole. Both he and Willie were relieved to get out with par. Only five holes to go.

Fourteen is almost a continuation of 13, a ribbon of fairway flanked by rugged sand dunes and played into a buffeting wind. Trying to relax as he walked to the tee, Kevin watched the seagulls, terns, and cormorants swooping and sailing and sweeping up toward billowing clouds. He took another Motrin, his third over the last six holes, and wondered if the capsules could also cause a numbing effect on his mind and body. Apparently not, because he hit another strong drive on the 388-yard par-4 hole. The low draw stayed below the worst of the wind and rolled an additional 50 yards after it hit the fairway. His 6-iron, however, wasn't as good and it caught the left greenside bunker. Kevin played a nice recovery shot, and then holed a windblown five-footer for par.

The 139-yard 15th is a harbinger of potential disaster ahead. It's perched on the westernmost tip of the Peninsula—atop an area known as Cypress Point—and the tee is just 25 feet above the Pacific. When the foursome got there, the surf was crashing onto the rocky shore below in a thunderous cadence, once with such force that Kevin felt a fine spray on his face. He was debating between hitting a 9-iron and a pitching wedge. The wind, which seemed to be blowing harder than it had all day, was crossing the hole from right to left. Kevin looked at Willie again.

"I prefer the wedge," Willie said. "But you'll need to hit it firm."

"I was thinking 9-iron."

"Pitching wedge."

Beyond a deep, narrow gorge, the small green is framed by bunkers and ice plant and overlooked by stunted evergreens and twisted, naked cypress trees. Kevin took his stance, closed the blade of the club slightly, aimed at the right bunker and punched the Titleist into the center of the green. No way was he going to charge the downhill putt. He crouched over it, making himself as small a target for the wind as possible. Still, a gust hit him the moment he stroked the putt and it caused him to shove the ball to the right of the cup. The tap-in kept him at four under par for the day and seven under for the tournament as he walked up to the 16th tee.

Over the last four hours, Kevin's round had taken on the aura of a drama. Subconsciously, his mind kept narrowing and narrowing its focus until Larry, the other two golfers and the fans existed only as shadowy bit players. All Kevin was aware of now was a green that was over 200 yards away and its fearsome protectors: the churning Pacific ahead of him, a rocky beach on the other side, a strong headwind, bunkers, and ice plant.

The tee is within shouting distance of 17-Mile Drive. It is hidden by trees and terrain, though. The only hint to motorists that one of golf's most valued treasures is sitting nearby are the man-made "No Trespassing" signs that are visible here and there.

The highway's name is a misnomer; it isn't even 17 miles long. Originally, it was—50 years ago—beginning and ending at the Del Monte Hotel in Monterey. But when the hotel became a Naval Postgraduate School, the scenic drive was shortened to 12 miles. Today, 17-Mile Drive loops from Carmel to Pebble Beach, through Cypress Point to Seal Rock and Bird Rock and Spanish Bay and into Pacific Grove. Its travelers marvel at the abundant wildlife, the architectural elegance of stately mansions, and the grandeur of rockbound coves, untamed seas and pristine forests.

The highway's most famous landmark is what's known as the Lone Cypress Tree. It's balanced atop a rocky outcropping protruding into the Pacific Ocean, and it's at the mercy of winds that should topple it and waves that should tear away its roots. Yet, as captured so magnificently in the painting by Willie's son, Ian, the Lone Cypress clings to its barren perch in proud defiance. It's the area's most photographed attraction.

Not far behind in shutterbug popularity is the 16th hole at

Cypress Point. Although protected from the general public, it has filled the viewfinders of countless sanctioned cameras. By far, it is the most photographed par-3 in the world. Golf dreamers by the thousands gaze at their own framed photos of the "16th at Cypress Point" and visualize themselves conquering this awesome adversary.

After his score matched the number of the hole in the 1953 Crosby, Porky Oliver's vision was a nightmare. He deposited five balls in the Pacific; the sixth became enmeshed in the ice plant. His travails became a topic of conversation at the tournament. When a San Francisco columnist saw him later that day, he said, "That was priceless, Porky old boy. Best laugh I've had in years." The glowering victim replied, "I guess you'd laugh at a broken leg."

Not that the 16th at Cypress is impregnable. In the 1982 tournament, touring pro Jerry Pate made a hole in one. But the hole's most memorable ace occurred late one autumn afternoon in 1947. Bing Crosby, playing in a friendly fivesome that included the club pro, peered at the distant target and considered his options. He finally decided to go for the green, and proceeded to fire a shot that was heard around the pubs and pro shops of the Monterey Peninsula for years afterward.

The 16th at Cypress Point measures 231 yards from the Championship markers. The teeing ground is on one promontory and the green is on another. In between, if played on a direct line, there are approximately 205 yards of Pacific Ocean and a cliff to carry. Ice plant at the top of the cliff also guards the putting surface, and the hole is always played into a strong wind.

There is, however, an alternate route to the 16th green, and that was what Kevin was considering as he stood on the tee.

To the left of the water, beginning within 50 yards of the tee, is a strip of fairway. Its only hazard is the stump of a dead cypress tree, but there is ample room on all sides of it. Compared to the appearance of the green, the fairway is a huge target—one that offers the possibility of making no worse than bogey and perhaps even a par. With the wind blowing as hard as it was, it was the smart way to go.

Without looking at Willie, Kevin pulled his driver out of the bag.

"Oh, lad, don't."

"I'm hittin' it good, Willie. I can make it."

Willie nodded. "'Tis true, you're in fine form," he said. "But you've been playing wisely, as well. Hogan was five below par the last time he reached this hole. He hit 5-iron to the fairway and still got his three."

Kevin tried to visualize hitting a shot to the bail-out area but couldn't. He could, however, clearly see the ball leaving his titanium driver on a low trajectory and boring through the wind and onto the green. Handing the driver's headcover to his caddie, he said, "Ben Hogan, I'm not."

After teeing the ball lower than he usually did, he also set up to the ball so that it was slightly further back in his stance. His only thoughts after that were to swing smoothly and to hit the hell out of it. Immediately following impact, there were excited shouts from the gallery.

"Yes!"

"Get there!"

The small, white sphere had rocketed off the tee like a guided missile, and Kevin knew he couldn't have struck it better. Teeing off on the first hole, instead of watching the flight of the ball, he had looked at his bandaged thumb. Now, holding his follow-through, he stared across the water...and held his breath.

The ball cleared the ice plant with inches to spare, skirted a bunker and rolled onto the front of the green. The fans packed around the tee erupted, whooping and hollering and drowning out the roar of the ocean. Larry shouted as loudly as anyone, before giving him both a high five *and* a low five. Lou Jackson and his partner offered congratulations. Only Willie was silent.

After Jackson played a safe shot to the fairway, the group headed forward to the tees that the amateurs would use. Thinking about what could have happened, Kevin shivered momentarily and his legs felt weak. Repeatedly reminding himself to *Hang in there, Kevin*, he managed to get his nerves under control by the time he got to the green. Putting firmly against the wind, he was amazed when the ball somehow stopped three feet short. He quickly decided not to wait, settled in over the ball, and calmly made the putt for par.

Although overshadowed by the breathtaking grandeur of the 16th, the 393-yard 17th at Cypress Point is considered by many critics to be the finest golf hole on the Monterey Peninsula. The elevated tee of the par 4 is located behind the 16th green. It's a dogleg to the right, requiring a drive over an inlet of the Pacific. The more of the inlet and the rocky coast the player bites off, the shorter the second shot will be. An intimidating cluster of black cypress trees, in the center of the fairway about a hundred yards from the green, adds to the challenge of the hole.

Kevin decided not to mess with the trees or again take liberties with the Pacific. He aimed well to the left and played a conservative 1-iron across a tiny portion of the inlet. It left him with a shot that once again needed to avoid the trees and the waiting water. After getting neither advice nor encouragement from Willie—his caddie hadn't said a world to him since the 16th tee—Kevin attempted to cut a 6-iron into the center of the green. The wind blocked the ball, however, and pushed it into a bunker to the left of the putting surface. Playing from the sand toward the ocean now, he hit a very careful shot that ended up eight feet above the cup. The wind blowing hard behind him, he carefully stroked the putt to within tap-in range and accepted his bogey five.

With a feeling of relief, Kevin turned away from the Pacific to play the inland 18th. He didn't need any more challenges. After again driving with his 1-iron, he then hit his approach into the center of the green and two-putted for his par. His score at Cypress Point was another 69.

Going over his card in the scorer's tent, Kevin held the short yellow pencil in his left hand because his right thumb was throbbing. Quietly, he thanked God that he didn't have to play another hole. Even out of the wind, he was suddenly cold and shivering. He felt exhausted but at the same time felt a great sense of satisfaction when he looked at his score. A 69 at Cypress Point in these conditions, under this much pressure and with a bad thumb? There was no way it could happen. He shook his head in wonder, because it had.

"Partner, we're only seven shots out of the lead," Larry said when Kevin emerged from the tent. "Sorry I didn't help you more. We'll make the cut, won't we?"

"I don't know," Kevin said, smiling. "Have to wait and see, I guess."

"Damn, we better. If I'd just made that putt on 17, you know? We better," he repeated. Larry told Kevin 'Great round,' gave him a high five, and said he was heading to the Tap Room for a drink.

Kevin smiled again as he watched him hurry away, then turned around and looked at the scoreboard. What Larry had failed to mention was that at six under par, Kevin was tied for second—one stroke behind a player at Spyglass Hill who still had seven holes remaining. The person Kevin was tied with, Kaori Noro, was just starting the back nine at Pebble Beach. There was at least a possibility that they'd be paired together in the final round.

Kevin noticed that Willie was standing off to the side of the scorer's tent with his golf bag, so he walked over.

"Shall I put your clubs in your car, Kevin, or the pro shop?"

Kevin? What happened to 'lad'?

"I didn't feel I was being stupid on 16, Willie. I was confident hitting my driver."

His lips in a fine line, Willie looked away.

"Do you understand what I'm saying?"

"Aye."

"Good, I'm glad."

Willie looked back at him. "Understanding isn't approving."

"But Willie, I parred the hole."

"Aye, and bogeyed the next."

"My score would have been the same, whether I went three-five or four-four."

"Even if you'd gone *one*-four," Willie said evenly, "the driver was the wrong club in that situation."

A Tour official suddenly interrupted them. "Excuse me, Kevin, same drill as yesterday. They're asking for you in the Media Center."

Kevin nodded, then looked back at Willie. "I am definitely

going to need your help tomorrow. But that doesn't mean that I'm always going to do what you say."

"Watson did," Willie said.

Kevin smiled and shrugged. "Well, I'm not Tom Watson, either. I'm just a club pro who happens to be playing well against the big boys. I shouldn't even be here...but I am. And you know what? I'm going to come out tomorrow and go at it the same way I did today, and yesterday, and the day before. If I fail," Kevin said, "it won't be the first time. But it also won't be because I didn't do everything I possibly could to win."

The Scotsman seemed on the verge of saying something but didn't.

Kevin said, "If you could drop my clubs off at the pro shop back at Pebble, I'd appreciate it. Thanks for your help today, Willie." He held out his hand and Willie took it. "You're a fine caddie."

Kevin turned around and headed for a courtesy car to take him to the Media Center.

Willie continued standing next to the upright golf bag and watched Kevin until he disappeared in the crowd of spectators. He then looked up at the scoreboard and stared at it for about 30 seconds. When he was done, he reached for the damp towel that was hung on the grip of Kevin's umbrella and began to carefully clean the faces of the clubs.

CHAPTER 8

Another player was being interviewed when Kevin wearily climbed the steps to the Media Center. He sat down on a chair in the back of the room and waited to be called. On the chair next to him was a newspaper opened to Dean Adams's morning column. Kevin couldn't wait to see who the prick was picking on today.

GOLF A GAME OF NOBILITY?
DON'T YOU BELIEVE IT!

Perhaps like you, I had been led to believe golf is the last bastion of integrity in sport. WRONG—at least judged by the antics of Kevin Courtney, head golf honcho at Pebble Beach.

Yesterday I reported how Courtney fired his caddie at Spyglass Hill and blamed his amateur partner, Mr. Larry Caldwell, for his own bad play, so upsetting Caldwell that he left the course without finishing the round. Their transgressions? The caddie asked another player in the foursome what club he used. Caldwell's supposed boo-boo—"seen" only by the eagle eye of Courtney—was to maybe touch a few grains of sand.

Yesterday, Mr. Caldwell again left the course upset and disillusioned. I wanted to know why, and asked him. It seems that on the 12th tee, Courtney looked in the golf bag of fellow-pro Lou Jackson to see what club he used. When Caldwell questioned Courtney about it, our local hero shrugged his shoulders and said, "Don't sweat it. The rules say it's okay."

Caldwell did sweat it, and so do I. Talk about your double standards...

Kevin thrust the paper aside. *Larry, Larry, Larry. No, don't blame it on Larry. Adams is the one distorting the whole thing.*

The other player's interview finished and Kevin was waved forward by the Communications Director. This time they wanted almost a hole-by-hole account of his round.

"You were four under going to 16," said Ray Bushfield of *Golfweek*. "Against that strong wind, did you even consider playing it safe?"

"Sure, I thought about it. But I'd driven it well all day, so..." He shrugged. "I was pretty sure I could make it."

"Hell of a shot," Bushfield murmured.

When the reporters' interest finally turned to his thumb, he told them he'd cut it opening a package. A writer wanted to know about the stitches, if they had affected his swing. "Only at first," Kevin replied.

"Not real smart to use something sharp when you're playing in a tournament, is it?" Adams asked.

Kevin shook his head. "No, it isn't. It's also a sure sign of a complete lack of integrity and decency."

There were a few snickers, then someone said, "Kevin, on the first day you had trouble with your caddie and your partner. After yesterday's round, you cut your thumb. Are you beginning to feel jinxed?"

Kevin shrugged again. "Luck is a big part of golf. Sometimes it's bad. But to tell you the truth, I feel pretty lucky to be where I am."

"You're only one shot off the lead. How do you explain your good play?"

"I don't have a clue," Kevin said. "It's as surprising to me as it must be to you people. As I said yesterday, I haven't been able to break an egg lately. So to break par twice in three days, well, it's simply a mystery."

"Planning to walk under any ladders?"

"No. Or go near a mirror, either."

A few minutes later, they let him go. He went down the stairs, heard someone behind him, and turned to see Dean Adams.

"One question, Courtney."

Kevin kept walking.

"What about the bet between you and Masaru Komoto?"

His heart suddenly beating faster, Kevin stopped and turned around again. There were other people nearby, and he didn't want Adams to shout anything else about the bet. "I don't know what you're talking about," he said as Adams came up to him.

"I hear he likes to bet on Noro."

"I wouldn't know."

Adams smiled. "You sure you don't have any bets going with Komoto this week?"

Kevin turned away and walked toward the giant scoreboard. When he got there, he was relieved to see that Adams hadn't followed him.

The player who was leading by one stroke when Kevin finished had bogeyed two holes coming in. Noro had a triple-bogey on the eighth hole, but had recovered well and was one under for the round with two holes to play. If he parred in, he would be tied with Kevin. That would mean they'd play in the final pairing on Sunday. Kevin headed for the pro shop, stopping numerous times to sign autographs. He had to hold the pencil awkwardly and it produced a scribble that was hardly legible. Kevin didn't care; his mind was elsewhere.

Jesus, how could Adams know about the bet? Komoto or Jack Leonard wouldn't have told him. But if he did know, why hadn't he blown the story wide open? It would be a hell of a scoop for any reporter, even a scumbag like Adams. Noro, maybe?

Kevin wasn't even sure that Noro knew about the bet.

The Japanese superstar had come into the pro shop on Tuesday for what was supposedly a courtesy call on the host pro. If he knew anything, he gave no hint.

"You are in tournament?" He was as tall as Kevin, but probably 20 pounds heavier. He radiated self-assurance.

"Yes."

"Never had opportunity to play with you, Kevin. Perhaps Sunday afternoon." He smiled. "But if you played Sunday afternoons, wouldn't have become club pro. Yes?"

Kevin had wanted to say, "Screw you, Bud." Instead, he said, "Yep. I'm afraid you're right about that."

A few minutes after Kevin arrived at his office, an assistant came in with the news that Noro had parred 17 and 18 for a 71. He was six under par for the tournament and tied with Kevin for the lead. The next day, the two of them would play in the last group.

Kevin spent about an hour with his staff, mostly going over sales figures and the shop's merchandise inventory. Amazed but proud that their boss was tied for the lead with the world's top-ranked player, they assured him that they could handle everything and encouraged him to go home and rest. Kevin did leave eventually, but he went to the hospital instead of home. He wanted to have his stitches checked.

"Like my golf game," he explained to Dr. Glouster when he saw him, "I need these sutures to hold together for one more day."

Glouster laughed, examined the cut, then told Kevin that everything looked great—even if he did say so himself. "And your game's going to hold up great tomorrow, too," he said. "I have a good feeling about that."

Walking out of the hospital 20 minutes later with a new bandage on his thumb, Kevin realized he still had time to go see Joey.

Driving to his ex-wife's house, he wondered again how much Dean Adams knew—and what the reporter might do about it. Was he saving it for his column in the morning? Or would he wait until tomorrow afternoon and try to get in front of the TV cameras? Kevin shook his head. The whole week had been full of questions, but with few answers.

Saturday was Joan's biggest real estate day. Joey usually had a sitter, an elderly neighbor who had come to the conclusion that Kevin was a child abuser. She often tried to prevent him from coming within 10 feet of his own son. But being elderly, she was pretty slow. Sometimes Joey would answer the door and they'd have a minute or two before she shuffled up and spoiled the get-together by glaring at Kevin.

He turned the corner onto Joan's street and saw Joey in the front yard, playing catch with a teenaged girl. For once, Kevin wouldn't even have to ring the doorbell.

"Dad!" Joey cried, running toward him as Kevin pulled to

the curb.

Kevin got out and walked around to the passenger side of the car. He knelt down and picked up his son. Joey hugged him tightly for a moment, then pulled back excitedly. "Me and Kelly are playing ball."

"I saw that. You guys having fun?"

Joey nodded vigorously.

"Hi, I'm Kelly," the girl said as she walked up. "You Joey's dad?"

"Yes, I'm Mr. Courtney. Nice to meet you, Kelly. Where's Mrs. Lundahl?"

"She's sick," Joey said.

Kevin looked at the girl. "Kelly, do you know when Joey's mother will be back?"

"She said around five. Six at the latest."

"Well, look. I know you're in charge, but do you think it would be okay if I took Joey to Cocogelato's for a little while?"

"Yes!" Joey cried. "Please, Kelly?"

Kevin said, "I promise I'll have him back by four-thirty."

"Well, I guess so," she said. "I do need to call a girl friend."

As they drove away, Joey said, "I like Kelly."

Kevin looked at his son, blond hair covering the tops of his ears. He had on jeans and a Forty-Niner sweatshirt. "Better than Mrs. Lundahl?"

"Yuck!"

Kevin laughed.

"Guess what, Dad?"

"What?"

"I got a hundred on a math test yesterday."

"That's great, Joey. I'm proud of you."

"What was your score?"

"Today? I had a 69."

"That's good, huh?"

"For me, it's very good."

"Dad? Mom said you'd rather play golf than be with me."

Kevin's fingers tightened on the steering wheel. "That's not true, Joey. There isn't anything more important to me than you. Even golf. It's just that I had to play in this tournament. When it's done, we're going to do a lot of stuff together. Okay?"

Joey smiled, nodded and said, "Okay."

Cocogelato was a well-known gourmet ice cream and confections café in downtown Carmel. Joey ordered a nutty rainbow cone; Kevin chose strawberry shortcake. They sat in a booth near the back of the store.

"What happened to your thumb, Dad?" Joey asked.

"Cut it on a razor blade."

"Wish I could shave."

"You will some day."

"I wish you still lived with us."

Kevin didn't respond.

"Tommy Thompson brought a frog to school."

"I bet your teacher loved *that*."

"Oh, Dad, guess what?"

"Can't guess."

"Some man came to see Mom yesterday and he talked like Mickey Mouse."

"Really?"

"He was big, too," Joey said. He tried to mimic the way the man had talked. "But he had this itty-bitty, squeaky voice." He giggled. "It was funny."

"Who was this guy?"

Joey shrugged his shoulders. "I dunno. Guess what?"

"Some girl kissed you."

Joey did a big, slow roll of his eyes. "No, Dad. I scored a *goal* yesterday."

"That's fantastic. Are you still playing right forward?"

Joey nodded, then wiped some ice cream off his chin with his napkin. "When can you come and watch me play?"

"Next week. And that's a promise."

"I'll score for you, Dad."

"I know you will."

Driving back to Joan's, Kevin found himself wondering if she had a new boyfriend. When they pulled up, Kelly was sitting on the front porch talking on a portable telephone. She finished her conversation and walked over to meet them.

"Play ball with us, Dad."

"Sorry, son, gotta go."

"I wish you could stay."

"I know. But I'm going to be here to pick you up early next Saturday morning, okay? We'll play ball...go to Cocogelato's ...see a movie...anything you want. Okay?"

"Okay."

Kevin said goodbye to Kelly and knelt down to give his son a hug. "Love you, pal."

"Love you, too, Dad."

Kevin had been going nonstop for 10 hours, but the adrenaline was still flowing. He went home, showered, and changed clothes. Forty minutes later he parked in front of the cottage in Pacific Grove. Willie answered the door after the first knock.

"It's gonna be a long night," Kevin said. "I could use a cup of coffee. Or something." He smiled.

Willie stepped back to let Kevin enter, then closed the door.

"I'm sorry, lad. I had no right to behave like a spoiled child today."

Kevin turned around to face him. "You were only doing your job."

"No, my job is to carry your clubs and offer advice when asked. You must play the shot as you see it."

"I guess we both have a bit of a temper."

"Aye, that we have," Willie said nodding. "I've yet to see a good player who isn't spirited."

"I hope you'll bring your spirit with you tomorrow."

"You still want me?"

"Willie, I *need* you."

The Scotsman hesitated momentarily, then nodded. "Thank you, lad."

"We'll be in the last group. Can you meet me in the pro shop at noon?"

"Aye."

Kevin patted Willie on the shoulder then started for the door.

"Can you come in for a minute or two, lad? There's something I would like to show you."

More of Ian's artwork?

As if he were reading Kevin's mind, Willie smiled and said, "It's about golf."

Ian's spotlighted painting was the first thing Kevin looked at when he and Willie entered the living room. He wondered if the light was ever turned off. Willie knelt in front of the fireplace, wadded up strips of newspaper and put them on the blackened grate. He then added kindling and two pieces of split firewood. Kevin watched him strike a match and hold it under the paper. It flamed up, casting a golden glow on Willie's face. The look of rejection he'd displayed on the tee of the 16th hole was no longer there. He seemed contented.

Apparently satisfied with his fire-making, Willie went to a bookcase across the room and opened a door at the bottom. He took out a large white box, then indicated for Kevin to sit on the sofa. Willie sat beside him, holding the box in his lap and meticulously removing four pieces of tape that held the lid in place. Slowly, he lifted it off.

Inside was a brown briefcase. It appeared to be old and made of leather. There were two straps with large brass buckles. Willie took the briefcase out of the box and with the same deliberate care that he used on the tape, he unfastened the buckles. A master magician couldn't have done a better job of piquing the interest of his audience. Yet, Kevin knew Willie wasn't putting on a show; the briefcase no doubt held a treasure that was very dear to him. For an instant, Kevin's eyes darted to the spotlighted Lone Cypress Tree.

Tentatively, Willie reached inside the briefcase and withdrew a white cloth that was wrapped by a rubber band. Removing the band, he unfolded the cloth—apparently a linen handkerchief—as if it encased the most fragile piece of art. What Willie uncovered, though, was an ordinary-looking white golf glove.

"For the Open in 1975," he said, looking at Kevin, "the 18th hole at Carnoustie was shortened from a par-5 to a long par-4. Jack Newton, the fine Australian player, appeared to be on his way to winning but bogeyed three of the last four holes. Watson and myself were several groups ahead. Tom was fortunate to make a long birdie putt on 18. As a result, he and Newton finished the 72 holes in a tie."

Kevin was listening intently, his eyes moving up and down from Willie's face to the white glove.

"Of course, they played off the following day," Willie said. "When Newton bunkered his second shot on 18, all Tom had to do to secure the Championship was get his approach somewhere on the green. There was a driving rain and the hole was playing much longer. Watson chose a 2-iron," Willie said, smiling. "Lad, I can still see that compact swing as if it were yesterday. The ball flew like an arrow, straight over the burn and into the middle of the green."

"The first of his five wins in The Open," Kevin murmured, his eyes now riveted on the white piece of leather.

"When he came off the green after putting-out for the win, he handed me his glove. Naturally, I started to put it in his bag. But Tom stopped me. He said, 'Willie, you keep it.'"

In spite of the heat from the fireplace, Kevin felt a chill go through him. "May I?" he asked.

Willie handed him the glove.

The leather was still soft and pliable, as if it were nearly new. Kevin pictured Watson standing there in the rain at Carnoustie, thousands of spectators packed in bleachers around the green and extending down both sides of the fairway in the tradition of The Open. He could see him tugging at his glove—this glove—before playing one of the great shots of his career. Of anyone's career.

"He must have thought a lot of you, Willie," Kevin said, handing back the glove.

"No, lad, I want you to have it."

"Absolutely not," Kevin protested. "This is a piece of golf history."

"Please."

The smile on Willie's face when he talked about the glove...the tenderness with which he handled it—no way could Kevin take that from him.

Leaving the glove on the sofa beside Kevin, Willie walked over to the painting. "If you would indulge me a few more minutes, I'd like to tell you about my son."

"Of course."

"I guess it was seven, eight years ago that he told us he was gay. His mother—she's been gone five years now, God rest her soul—accepted it completely. I couldn't." Willie smiled faintly. "One of my many flaws. Anyhow, Ian had a studio in our house when she died. He was our only child, all I had. But I still wasn't able to deal with the situation. He sensed this, felt he wasn't welcome there, so he left six months after his mother's death."

Kevin had moved to the edge of the sofa.

"Ian came to Pacific Grove. He had a friend who had come a year earlier. They shared this house. He wrote to me, excited about all the galleries and his opportunities to paint and to sell his work. Every Christmas he sent a card. I never replied. Finally, I suppose, he gave up trying to communicate with me. Two years ago, I received a letter from a lady who helped people with AIDS. Ian had the disease. His friend had died and Ian was living here alone."

Willie paused, took out a handkerchief and dabbed at his eyes. Kevin got up and put an arm around his shoulders.

"That's when I realized how much I had hurt us both," Willie said. "But it was too late by then. I telephoned Ian and asked if I could come and see him. He should have hung up the phone. But he said I could, so I came and stayed with him until he died."

They turned to face Ian's painting. For several seconds the only sound was the crackling of the burning logs. Then, squeezing the old Scotsman's shoulders, Kevin said, "You were here when Ian needed you the most. That must have meant a lot to him, having his father here...knowing you accepted him."

"You're too kind, lad," he said. He walked over to the sofa and picked up the glove. "Ian was twelve when I caddied at Carnoustie. He played a bit of golf, but I hoped he'd learn to love it some day. I planned to give this to him when he got older." He shrugged, then held out the glove toward Kevin. "It would make me happy if you had it."

"But..."

"Please, Kevin."

Earlier in the day, Willie had called him by his given name in anger. This time it was done with affection. Kevin accepted the gift. "Thank you."

Willie shook his head. "I should be thanking you, lad."

A grandfather clock in a corner of the room began to chime the hour.

"Can you stay for supper?" Willie asked. "I have Scotch broth on the stove."

"Thanks, but I already have plans," Kevin said. "How about a rain check?"

"Any time, lad," Willie replied. He walked with Kevin to the door.

"Oh, before I forget," Kevin said, "I'm going to have some-one pick you up in the morning so you don't have to ride your bike."

"Thanks, but I like to bicycle. Fine exercise."

"But..."

"Don't worry, I'll be there on time. You just make sure that you get some rest."

Kevin grinned. "Don't want me to be too tired to lift that

big driver of mine tomorrow?"

"No, lad," Willie said. "I don't want you to be too tired to lift that big *trophy* tomorrow."

CHAPTER 9

After leaving Pacific Grove, Kevin drove back to Pebble and quickly made his pilgrimage to the 18th tee. When he got back, he went into the pro shop and picked out a new shirt and sweater to wear the next day. He saw Jack Leonard briefly. The Director of Golf congratulated him on how well he was playing, considering all the pressure. "Although," he said, in his always-surprising, high-pitched voice, "it's nothing compared to what you'll feel tomorrow. Good luck with it."

Kevin thanked him and headed for home as quickly as he could. Leonard's phony sincerity had pissed him off. He fumed about it all the way to the condo, during his shower, and while he dressed in a sport coat and tie. Driving to the party at the palatial home of the Osbornes—overlooking Pebble's 14th fairway—he tried to put Jack Leonard out of his thoughts.

When Bing Crosby brought his tournament to the Monterey Peninsula, the social activities became as important as the golf. For many residents of the Carmel/Pebble Beach area, golf actually takes a back seat to the parties—or the "clambakes" as they are called. As soon as the Pro-Am is over, they begin planning how to make next year's bashes even bigger and better.

There are countless gatherings. A San Francisco newspaper once observed, "A French election doesn't have as many parties." Why they are called "clambakes" is anybody's guess—not even Crosby could explain it. Very possibly it's because the revelers in the early days entertained on the beach below their seaside homes in Del Mar, La Jolla, Oceanside, and San Clemente.

Kevin expected the huge front door to be opened by a butler or maid. Instead it was Ruth Osborne, wearing a black cocktail dress, a pearl necklace, and diamond bracelets on both wrists.

"Kevin! I'm so thrilled you could make it." She gave him a little hug and pressed her right cheek against his. "I was afraid that since you're leading the tournament...I mean, I'm glad you're leading, but I thought..."

Kevin laughed. "Would you like to take a mulligan, Ruth?"

Ted Osborne, in a tuxedo, suddenly appeared in the doorway. He extended his hand "What my wonderful wife means, Kevin, is congratulations on your play and thanks for coming."

Kevin shook with his left hand. "Thanks for inviting me."

The couple ushered him inside. "Sometime tonight," Ted said, "I'd like for you to take a look at my grip. I'm hitting a lot of hooks lately."

"For God's sake, Ted, let the man relax."

"You're absolutely right, dear." Ted winked at Kevin and gently took his arm. Ruth took the other one and they escorted him from the entrance hall into a room that seemed as long as a short par 3. Kevin was aware of beams, rafters, and joists; massive windows overlooking illuminated grounds; and scores of people dancing, sitting at round tables, or standing in small clusters. A small combo that was set up in one corner of the room was playing an early Eagles' song.

Ruth waved at the band's leader and gestured for them to stop playing. She then got the attention of the guests.

"I'll make this short and sweet, so you can get back to whatever sinful things you were doing. This is Kevin Courtney, our fabulous pro here at Pebble Beach. As I'm sure most of you know, Kevin is tied for the lead in the Pro-Am. Tomorrow he's going to win it!" Following prolonged cheers, whistles, and applause, she continued. "Now that we've all welcomed our conquering hero, let's continue to enjoy the clambake. And, please, let's not besiege Kevin. He wants to enjoy the party, too. Enjoy!"

"What would you like from the bar?" Ted asked. "Beer, wine, champagne, soda? A cocktail?"

"Coors would be fine, if you have it."

"If we don't, we'll damn well get it. C'mon."

It took a few minutes to reach the bar at the far end of the room. People patted Kevin on the back, congratulated him on his score and wished him well in the next day's round. The bar was adorned with golf clubs and towels. Multicolored golf umbrellas served as a canopy.

After getting their drinks, the two men made their way through the crowd toward one of the large living room windows.

Many of the backyard trees were spotlighted; more subtle illumination displayed bushes and gardens. Beyond the foliage, Kevin knew, was the fairway of the par-5 14th hole.

Nearly shouting because of the noise, Ted said, "I've been watching the pros play this hole for eight years, Kevin. Almost every one of them lays up with his second shot so he can have about a hundred yards to the green. Leaves you with a sand wedge for your third, and a much better chance of stopping it on the top tier where the pin is always located on Sunday. Am I right?"

Kevin nodded.

"Okay now," Ted said, "something else I've noticed is that with the wind behind you on that third shot—like it will be tomorrow because there's a storm coming in—there's almost no way in hell to keep the ball from going over the green from a hundred yards out. Tomorrow—if you hit a good drive on 14, and I'm sure you will—think about hitting everything you've got on your second shot. Aim a little left, and the chances are good you'll either be in the bunker or light rough. Fairly simple shot from either spot. If you don't make birdie, it's a sure par. Hmm?"

"Not a bad plan," Kevin said.

"There you are," Ruth said, suddenly appearing through the crowd of guests. "Darling, didn't you hear my lecture about giving Kevin some space?"

"Just giving him a little tip, my love, that's all."

"Wonderful," Ruth said dryly. "He's leading the tournament, and *you're* giving him tips. Ted, we want him to *win* this thing."

"Actually, Ruth," Kevin said, smiling, "it was a good suggestion."

"Yeah, well, did Nicklaus, here, suggest trying our lovely buffet?"

"I was just about to do that," Ted said.

"Uh-huh." Ruth took Kevin's arm. "Come on, Kevin, let me save you from this person."

Under Ruth's guidance now, Kevin suspected her cuisine would be slightly more elaborate than Willie's Scotch broth. He was right. The food was arranged like a miniature golf course, 18 holes made of green felt—tees and fairways and greens. Toy trees lined the fairways; beige felt bunkers protected the greens. Each fairway was loaded with food. There was caviar and shrimp and lobster tail and oysters on the half-shell. There were little drumsticks and meatballs and more varieties of canapés than Kevin could count. Plus, cheese balls with fancy crackers, every conceivable fruit and vegetable, crepe suzettes, eclairs, and countless other foods he couldn't begin to identify.

Kevin hoped the party would help get his mind off the next day's round, would relieve some of the anxiety starting to gnaw at his gut. It wasn't working, though, and he wondered how many gourmet delicacies his stomach could handle.

"You don't want to miss this," Ruth said, pointing to a tray of food, "and those over there are to *die* for."

By the time he reached the sixth hole, Kevin knew there was no way he could even eat half of what he had on his plate.

"Your course is too long for me, Ruth. We'd better stop."

"I should have started more people on the back nine," she said with a sigh.

One of the guests called Ruth's name so she excused herself to Kevin. Moments later, a maid approached him. "Sir, the gentleman in the corner to your left would like you to join him."

Masaru Komoto was sitting alone, holding one of the single red roses that were used to decorate each table. Kevin was aware of other places to sit, but suddenly decided to confront the man he was sure was responsible for the two-stroke penalty and his cut thumb. Certain that Komoto wouldn't dare do anything in front of witnesses, Kevin walked over to the table.

Smiling, still holding the rose, the owner of Pebble Beach stood and bowed. "Ah, Mr. Courtney, I am honored that you have accepted my invitation. Please be seated."

Indicative of his stature, Komoto's private table was separated from the others. *Wouldn't want to get too close to common millionaires, now would we?* Kevin thought. He took the chair opposite Komoto.

"Are you enjoying yourself, Mr. Komoto?" Kevin asked pleasantly.

"Yes, thank you," Komoto replied. "It's a nice home and a nice party."

"Oh, I'm not talking about the party."

Komoto stared at Kevin for a moment then shook his head. "Unfortunately, Mr. Courtney, I sometimes do not understand the English language. Explain, please."

Kevin smiled then took a sip of his beer. "Well, let's see. First, you bribe my caddie to cause me a two-shot penalty. Then someone sticks a razor blade on my car door so that I cut my thumb. Must be annoying that I'm still in the tournament, huh?"

"I noticed your bandage while you were getting your food," Komoto said. "Bribe a caddie? I know nothing about such a thing. Since we met at Jack's last Monday, I have been in Las Vegas on business. I returned this afternoon."

Kevin shrugged. "Oh, I'm sure you have lots of associates who'll do your little dirty tricks for you."

Immaculate in a gray suit, white shirt, and gray and blue tie, Komoto frowned. "You talk in riddles, Mr. Courtney."

Kevin wiped his lips with his napkin before he spoke.

"Yeah, well," he said, "it's better than dealing in lies."

"Lies?" Komoto asked softly. He looked off for a moment, then picked up a fork and made several tracings on the linen tablecloth. For a while, he seemed to be studying them. "When I am puzzled, I often find understanding in a Japanese proverb: 'Beneath a giant tree lies the unseen root.' The unseen root is that you believe I arranged various incidents to prevent you from defeating Kaori?"

"Who else? If I fail, you win. It's as simple as that, isn't it?"

"There are other people, Mr. Courtney," Komoto said, "who would benefit from a transformation of Pebble Beach."

"But not as much as you," Kevin replied. "Not by a long shot."

"I see." Komoto took a sip of wine, then carefully set the glass on the table. "In your Christian Bible, St. Matthew cautions not to strain at a gnat and swallow a camel. We Asians have a proverb that conveys a similar thought: 'He eats an elephant, and is suffocated with a gnat.'"

Kevin wasn't sure he'd ever seen eyes as intent as the dark pair he was staring into across the table.

"The value of the Pebble Beach property," Komoto continued, "is several hundred million dollars. My net worth is several *billion*. If I don't sell it, it will be nothing more than a momentary irritant. I boasted of Kaori Noro, and you—as you Americans say—'called me on it.' I admired you for quickly offering me a challenge I could not refuse. Without challenges, life would be less interesting, don't you agree? It stimulates us, and it can give us worth—self-worth—if we are successful." He paused. "But only, Mr. Courtney, if we are honorable in the attempt."

Kevin continued staring at Komoto, trying to weigh what

he was hearing against the week's actual happenings.

"I see by your expression," Komoto said, "that doubt has replaced disgust. I am pleased. Now let me offer you further assurance. If Pebble Beach were worth 50 billion dollars, I still would do nothing dishonest to keep you from defeating Kaori. I have a reputation for integrity that I value more than my wealth. I'm certain you have a personal code of ethics; so do I."

"Did you tell Noro of the agreement?"

"Yes, I thought it only fair that he know. However, I demanded his pledge of secrecy. As the greatest golfer in the world, I am sure he was certain that he would defeat you. In spite of your excellent play, I am equally certain he is still confident of victory. As you said moments ago, 'It is as simple as that.'"

Kevin stared unblinking at the owner of Pebble Beach, searching for a sign that would confirm his thoughts over the past several days. Seeing none, he extended his left hand across the table. "I would like to apologize for my accusations."

Komoto bowed his head briefly before he reached for Kevin's hand. "Your apology is accepted, Mr. Courtney. May the best man win."

Kevin had barely touched his food but he now felt tired rather than hungry. He excused himself, found Ruth, and thanked her for a nice time. He told her he needed to get some rest.

"Where can I find Ted?"

"Try the front door. I think a guest just arrived."

It was a woman, her back to Kevin as she talked to Ted. Her black hair was cut short. When she turned her head to survey the party, Kevin saw who it was.

"Hello, Sara."

"You two know each other?" Ted asked, surprised. "Damn, I was getting ready to make glowing introductions."

"Hello, Kevin," Sara said without emotion.

"I hope you're not going already, Kevin," Ted said. "We're just getting started."

"I know. Any other time…"

Osborne nodded and extended his hand. "Good luck tomorrow. We'll be rooting like hell for you."

"Thanks." Kevin watched him walk into the party, then looked back at Sara.

She was wearing a red sequined cocktail dress and was staring at the bandage on his hand. "Did that happen yesterday?"

"Yeah."

"After I left you by the pro shop?"

"Yep."

"Looks professionally bandaged. Stitches?"

"Oh, yeah."

Sara eyed him for a few moments. "Is that why you rang my doorbell at ten after nine last night?"

Kevin nodded. "I didn't have a chance to call you from the hospital. And when I finally got out of there, my car phone was dead. I figured you got ticked-off when I didn't show up, and decided to do something without me."

Sara's shoulders slumped. "Shit. I had everything we needed: steaks, wine. All I had to do was answer the door. Sorry."

"No reason to be. I was the one who was two hours late. *I'm* sorry I gave up and went home."

Sara smiled. "I had planned to watch you play, today," she said. "Instead, I spent the whole day in the office working on a brief."

"Probably saved you from getting pneumonia."

She looked at his bandage again. "So how'd that happen?"

"A razor blade was taped to the door handle when I went out to drive to your place."

"Good God, Kevin. I thought golf was just a game."

"Apparently not to everybody."

"Komoto, you think?"

"I thought so at first," Kevin said, "but I just talked to him and I don't think he had anything to do with it. Or paying off little Brucie, either."

Sara looked puzzled. "Then who?"

"Your guess is as good as mine. Probably better."

They were quiet for a moment. Then Sara said, "How in the world did you manage to get in the lead with that thumb?"

"Also a mystery," Kevin replied.

"What about tomorrow?"

Kevin shrugged. "Tee it up, go find it, hit it again. Low score wins."

"Do you feel good about it?"

"Yeah," he said, nodding. "I mean, I've made it this far, so why not go all the way? You know?"

She smiled again. "I like that answer. Okay if I come out and watch?"

"Absolutely."

"Good. Then I'll see you tomorrow."

"Okay. Have fun tonight." Before leaving, he watched her walk down the hall into the party.

On the way home, he wished he'd told her how wonderful she looked.

CHAPTER 10

At first Kevin thought it was thunder. As it continued, though, rudely dragging him from the blessed refuge of sleep, he realized someone was pounding on the front door of his condo. He raised his head off the pillow and squinted at the end table next to his bed. His alarm clock read 6:03. Now the doorbell was chiming.

"What the hell?"

He turned on the bedside lamp, got up and slipped on a pair of pants, then went to the door. The wide-angle lens of the peephole distorted the images and gave them a surrealistic form. Or were they supposed to be that way because he was still asleep and this was a dream?

He pulled his head back when the pounding began again, then looked out when there was a pause. A man's face was momentarily inches from his. Then it, too, pulled back. Behind him, another man held a video camera with lights. Even farther in the background was a van with a huge 8 painted on the side. It was clearly a news crew from a local TV station.

"What the hell do you want?" Kevin shouted through the door.

"Kevin Courtney?"

"Yeah, what do you want?"

"To talk to you."

"Get out of here or I'm gonna call the police!"

"Won't do you any good," the man yelled back.

Kevin paused and tried to think. "All right, but turn off the lights and the camera."

The man looked behind him and said something that Kevin couldn't hear. Then the bright lights went out, leaving only the illumination of the carriage lamps on either side of the door. Kevin unlocked the door and opened it as far as the security chain allowed.

"Skip DeWall, Channel Eight News," the first man said. "Like to ask you about your agreement with Mr. Komoto."

Kevin had known it the moment he looked through the peephole. Still, he couldn't believe it actually was happening. "I don't know what you're talking about."

"That he won't sell Pebble Beach to developers if you beat Kaori Noro."

Kevin looked from the first man to the second, then back again. "Do your mothers know what you slimeballs do for a living?"

"This may refresh your memory," the reporter replied. He stuck a folded newspaper through the opening in the door and Kevin took it. Unfolding the paper, he saw an old PGA Tour photo of himself and a headline that read:

Pebble Beach Future Resting On
Courtney's Shoulders

A small picture of Dean Adams topped the article below

the headline, along with his byline.

Host professional Kevin Courtney is playing for more than the first prize check of $200,000 in today's final round of the AT&T Pebble Beach National Pro-Am. This reporter has learned of a secret agreement between Courtney and Masaru Komoto, owner of Pebble Beach, that the facility will be sold to a real estate developer if Courtney fails to defeat Japanese star Kaori Noro in today's fourth round. At the end of yesterday's third round, the two players were tied for the lead at six under par.

When Komoto made the agreement...

Sickened that what he had feared had actually come true, Kevin handed the paper back to the reporter.

"Care to respond, Mr. Courtney?"

Kevin was silent.

"Mr. Courtney?"

"No comment."

"Where did this meeting with Komoto take place?"

"No comment."

"This isn't being taped," the reporter said. "It's strictly off the record, so..."

Kevin shut the door and watched through the peephole as the reporter said something to his cameraman. Both men looked at the door again, then turned and went back to their vehicle. Beyond them, another van drove into the parking lot, this one labeled on the side with a huge 46. Kevin went to get the piece of paper with Sara's telephone number on it and called her from the kitchen.

"Hullo."

"It's Kevin, Sara. Sorry to wake you, but I've got an emergency."

"What's wrong?"

"That jerk Dean Adams found out about the bet with Komoto somehow and wrote about it in today's paper. I've got a couple of news crews camped in my parking lot."

"Have you talked to them?"

"I told them 'no comment.'"

"No one ever got hurt by *that* answer." She made little grunting sounds as if she was sitting up in bed or rolling over to a more comfortable position. "Seems to me that this is a Tour problem. Don't they have someone who deals with the media?"

"Oh, shit," Kevin said. "Of course they do. I'm so sorry to have bothered you, Sara. I'll call Richard Gardner right now."

"If he can't help you, call me back."

"You still coming today?" He heard her begin to yawn and waited for it to finish.

"Wouldn't miss it," Sara said. "Okay if I wear my new Donna Karan hotshot attorney outfit?"

Kevin smiled. "Sure, but leave the heels at home. Nikes would be a lot more comfortable."

"Got it."

"There'll be a pass at 'Will Call' for you."

"Thanks."

"Go back to sleep."

"Okay. Kevin?"

"Yeah?"

"Beat his butt."

Kevin hung up and was wondering how to reach the Tour's Director of Communications when the phone rang. The kitchen clock showed 6:21. He decided that only some local newsperson would call at that early hour. He let it ring as long as he could stand it but finally picked up the receiver. It was

Richard Gardner.

"Hello, Richard," Kevin said pleasantly. "Getting ready for your morning run?"

"Well, I'm glad somebody is finding all of this funny," Gardner replied. He didn't sound happy but he didn't sound angry, either.

"If it would help to cry," Kevin said, "I'd do it. But I don't think it will."

"How 'bout swimming in shark infested waters?"

"Can't swim."

"Even better."

"Oh, *that's* nice," Kevin said. "Some comfort you are."

"Kevin, is this true? This agreement with Komoto?"

"Yes."

"Unbelievable." Gardner sighed heavily. "Do me a favor and tell me exactly how this came about."

Kevin told him about the meeting with Komoto at Jack Leonard's house. When he finished, Gardner said, "Did you tell Dean Adams about it?"

"You kidding? The *last* thing I wanted was for this to get out. I figured Komoto would back out of the bet if it did. Now," Kevin said, "thanks to that asshole Adams, I've got news guys on my doorstep."

"I'm not surprised. I've heard from *Sports Illustrated*, ESPN, *The New York Times*, some London paper, Japanese television, all the major California papers...and the list is growing by the minute. It's pretty crazy, and it's going to get worse if we don't handle it right."

Kevin cursed himself for not spending the night at The Lodge. The media probably wouldn't have found him there.

"Here's what I think we should do, Kevin. Your tee time is

12:14. How much time do you need to warm up?"

"If you're about to ask me to talk to the media, forget it."

"Don't do this to me, Kevin," Gardner said. "This could be the golf story of the decade and you cannot stonewall it. We've got to give them something."

"Richard, it'll be a circus."

"Better a circus than a revolt that may completely disrupt the tournament. You don't want newspeople yelling questions at you in the middle of a swing, do you? If we don't give them something beforehand, they'll do it. Believe me."

Kevin sighed in resignation.

"Ten minutes, Kevin, that's all I ask."

"All right, all right. But I want at least an hour to warm up."

"No problem. We'll meet with the media at 10:45. I'll read a statement, we'll let them ask a few questions, and then we'll cut it off."

"Will Komoto be there? And Noro?"

"I hope to have them both."

"I still say it's going to be a circus."

"We'll try to prevent that with additional security and by keeping it short," Gardner replied. "The golf writers still have to cover the tournament and they have deadlines to meet. If they delay play too much, they'll be *working* at midnight instead of partying. *That* they'll avoid like the plague. It's going to be all right. Okay?"

"Okay, Richard," Kevin said, "I'll leave it in your hands. I'll see you at 10:45."

"Great, thanks," Gardner said. "Now go back to sleep." He hung up the phone.

Kevin thought: *Yeah, right.*

CHAPTER 11

Kevin told the reporters out front about the 10:45 press briefing, unplugged his phone, then went back to bed. He stared at the ceiling and began playing Pebble Beach in his head. After a few holes, he decided that this was a bad idea. *Don't plan, just play,* he thought. *One swing at a time, one hole at a time.*

Tom Watson's golf glove was on the nightstand, still wrapped in Willie's handkerchief. Kevin turned his head to look at it. He wondered what Watson had done to handle the pressure that day at Carnoustie. How he had managed to hit that 2-iron through the rain and onto the 18th green to win his first British Open. Was his swing so grooved that it was immune to the enormity of the occasion? Probably no swing ever was, Kevin decided, especially when trying to win something as big as The Open—or to save Pebble Beach. But still, Watson had to have had faith in his swing and in himself to pull it off. Kevin remembered something he had said to Sara the night before. *I've made it this far, so why not go all the way?*

That was faith in himself, sort of, wasn't it?

He looked at his alarm clock. It had crawled to 7:15. He fixed a cup of instant coffee, took it back to bed, propped himself up with a pillow, turned on his small TV and surfed through the programs. Eventually, he settled on an old Randolph Scott movie called "The Tall T." Kevin knew that Scott had played a lot of golf at Pebble Beach during the 1940s and '50s and had heard that he was a pretty good amateur. He tried to picture the cowboy on the screen swinging a golf club, but couldn't.

The alarm was set to go off at 9:00 a.m. Kevin turned off the TV, rolled onto his side, stayed there for less than a minute before rolling to the other side, then was on his back staring at the ceiling again. Suddenly, he was startled by a sharp noise. This time it *was* thunder, and moments later rain started beating against the bedroom windows. He glanced at the clock again: 8:12. It was exactly four hours until his tee time. He got out of bed and switched off the alarm button.

After his shower, Kevin put on a pair of beige slacks and the blue shirt and sweater he'd picked out at the pro shop. He stuck Watson's glove in one of his back pockets, planning to transfer it to his golf bag later for good luck.

The rain had stopped by the time he left the condo. The sun was peeking out from behind a cloud, the TV crews were gone, and mission bells were chiming in the distance. Except for the tournament, it was a typical peaceful Sunday morning in Carmel, California. Kevin stood outside the front door for nearly a minute, his eyes sweeping the parking area for anything suspicious. Seeing nothing unusual, he walked to the Riviera and looked it over closely. He took deep breaths, hoping the surrounding serenity would somehow enter his body and take control.

It didn't.

On his way to the course, Kevin passed by his usual breakfast stop. Butterflies were assembling in his stomach and the thought of food nearly made him nauseous. Even the coffee in his travel mug tasted lousy.

There are five access spots to 17-Mile Drive and each includes a booth for collecting the fee it costs to travel the scenic route. The closest entrance for Kevin was Carmel Hill gate, just off Highway 1. He was sure that the tournament would cause a minor slowdown at all of gates that morning, so he was glad that the employee sticker on his windshield enabled him to use a special lane.

Minor turned out to be an understatement. Five blocks from the Carmel Hill gate, in spite of the unpredictable weather, cars were backed up bumper-to-bumper. Kevin eased into the employee lane and began to move past them. At the tollbooth, an elderly guard glanced at his car and appeared ready to signal him through. Instead, he began waving frantically for him to stop. Kevin lowered his window.

"You're gonna win today, son!" the guard shouted. "We're all behind you!"

As he joined a new procession of cars creeping along the winding road to Pebble Beach, Kevin wondered if he would be worthy of the guard's confidence. "Positives, Kevin," he suddenly said out loud. "Positives. Only…positives." He turned on the car's radio and began to search for a song that might inspire him. He also kept checking the time.

At 10:30, he knew there was no way he was going to make it in time for the press conference. He phoned the pro shop and asked his top assistant to let Richard Gardner know he was going to be late.

"Not necessary," Jerry said. "They pushed everything back an hour because of the storm. The press conference is now at 11:45. You go off at 1:12."

"Any damage to the course?"

"A couple of the new trees got blown around a little, but nothing major. Mr. Leonard had a huge cypress come down, though. Right in front of the garage. His wife can't get her car out. Hey, Kevin?"

"Yeah?"

"I can't believe this thing with you and Mr. Komoto. Is it really true?"

"'Fraid so, Jerry."

"Shee-it," Jerry said. "Am I glad I'm not in your shoes."

Kevin finally passed the 14th green and turned off 17-Mile Drive toward his reserved parking place. He wasn't able to park the car, though, until two sheriff's deputies moved a crowd of spectators and newspeople out of the way. They also had to escort him to the pro shop.

"Go get 'em, Kevin!"

"You can do it!"

Several news reporters, walking backward, shoved microphones in his face and shouted questions that he couldn't understand or couldn't answer. *How the hell am I supposed to know if I'm going to beat Noro today? We haven't played yet.*

Reaching the main entrance finally, Kevin practically pushed his way into the pro shop. There were customers everywhere. The deputies immediately began to clear a path to his office as people shouted encouragement to him. Several even reached out to him, as if he were some rock star. Motioning to his top assistant to follow him, Kevin finally reached the sanctuary of his office.

"What the hell is going on out there?" Kevin asked.

"Best I can tell," Jerry said, "is that all these people are expecting you to get your ass beat today. Therefore, we'll be closing soon and this may be their last chance to get a souvenir from Pebble Beach. At this rate, we'll be sold out of everything in a couple hours."

"It's nice to know that they have so much faith in my ability," Kevin said sarcastically. "Makes me feel *really* good."

"Look on the bright side," Jerry said, grinning. "You might *lose* Pebble Beach, but you may *win* 'Merchandiser of the Year.'"

Kevin laughed. "You're a big help, too, you know that?"

"Listen, Kevin," Jerry said. "I've played a lot of golf with you, and I know your game as well as anybody. If you can get it going, you can beat this guy."

"*If* I get it going," Kevin replied.

"You've done it before. I was with you when you shot that 65 here, and it was blowing pretty good that day. Remember?"

Kevin nodded. "Yeah, I remember."

"Good. Make sure you *keep* remembering it. All the way around."

"I will," Kevin said. "Thanks, Jerry." He turned to look through his office window at the crowd of customers, then looked back at his assistant.

"Have you seen my caddie?"

"By the putting green."

"Ask him to come in, will you? And do me a favor and take a VIP badge over to 'Will Call' for me."

"You got it," Jerry said. He opened the office door. "What name should I put on the envelope for the badge?"

"Sara Arnold. S,a,r,a."

While he waited for Willie, Kevin removed an extra sweater and a box of balls from the big pouch on his golf bag. He then put the glove that Watson had worn at Carnoustie in their place.

"Good morning, lad."

"Morning, Willie," Kevin said, standing up. "How're you feeling after your bike ride in?"

The old Scotsman smiled. "Fit as a fiddle, and rarin' to go." He was wearing the same blue tam he'd worn the day before. White tufts of hair were sticking out everywhere. He also had on a pair of tan corduroys, tennis shoes, and a warm-looking, navy nylon windbreaker with a Carnoustie logo on the left breast.

"I assume you've heard about my agreement with Mr. Komoto by now?"

"Aye. We're going to win. I can feel it in my bones."

"Well at least we've got a chance, Willie," Kevin said. "And that's all any pro wants on the last day: a chance. Have a seat and relax while I meet with the media for a few minutes. Then we'll go hit some balls and warm up."

The office door opened and Richard Gardner walked in. He said, "Good morning," introduced himself to Willie, then asked Kevin if he had a copy of the agreement.

Kevin had taken it out of the console after he'd parked the car. He handed the folded paper to the Director of Communications.

"You're kidding me," Gardner said. "This is it?"

"The whole thing."

Gardner read through it. "Pretty damn crude, if you ask me."

"My attorney says it's legal, though."

"So does Mr. Komoto. I talked to him about it a few minutes ago."

Kevin felt a sense of relief. Ever since Monday, he'd been half expecting Komoto to find a way to back out of the bet.

"Okay, my friend," Gardner said, handing the paper to Kevin, "here's the deal. Both Komoto and Noro declined to meet with the media. But Jack Leonard said he'd be there."

It didn't surprise Kevin that the two Japanese would choose to ignore the circus. It would also allow Noro additional practice time. Leonard, no doubt, would somehow try to gloss over Komoto's attempt to destroy one of golf's shrines. Probably by reminding everyone that America was a free country and that a man could sell one of his possessions if he wanted to. Kevin hoped Jack would use those exact words; the media would eat him alive.

"I'll read the agreement, what there is of it," Gardner said, "then I'll open it up for questions."

"Remember, Richard, I'm out of there in 10 minutes."

"I know, I know. C'mon, let's get going."

They left Kevin's office and made their way through the crowded pro shop. Besides the deputies, several Tour officials helped escort Kevin and Gardner to the upstairs Media Center. There were at least a hundred people waiting inside, most facing a lectern that stood in front of three chairs.

Jack Leonard was sitting in one of them. He glanced up at Kevin as he arrived at the front of the room, nodded, then quickly averted his eyes. Kevin sat down. The rear and one side of the room were lined with TV cameras. There appeared to be a dozen microphones attached to the lectern, and almost as many tape recorders on the floor next to it.

Dean Adams was sitting in the front row, smiling for a change. He was obviously pleased with himself for placing the ultimate obstacle in Kevin's path: millions of golfers all over the world were depending on Kevin to save Pebble Beach.

Earlier, Kevin had tried to figure out who had told Adams about the bet. But now it didn't matter. Knowing that person's name would not change anything, and it would definitely not make what he had to accomplish any easier.

After Gardner read the agreement between Kevin and Komoto to the media, he emphasized to them that there would only be a few minutes for questions and answers, then gestured for Kevin to come up to the lectern.

"Kevin, how long have you known about the plan to turn Pebble Beach into a real estate development?"

"I learned about it last Monday."

"How?"

"I'm not at liberty to say."

"From Komoto?"

"No, but he did confirm what I had heard."

"Is that when you made the bet?"

"Yes."

"What happens if someone else wins the tournament?"

"Doesn't matter," Kevin replies, shaking his head. "The bet is based on whether I beat Noro or he beats me."

"What made you think you could beat the world's best golfer when you haven't played competitively for over a year?"

Kevin smiled. "What makes you think I *thought* I could beat him?" The reply caused some laughter in the crowd. "Look. When all this happened, all I did was try to think of a way to stop the development of Pebble Beach. It was one of those spur of the moment things; the bet was the first thing I thought of." He shrugged. "If I'd been smarter, I would've bet Mr. Komoto that I could beat Noro in a two-mile run. Kaori is not exactly what I'd call 'petite.'"

Even more of the reporters laughed.

"You've still got a chance to beat him," one of them said.

"Yes," Kevin said, "and that's really all I was hoping for. Golf is a funny game, and none of us really know what's going to happen until we put it in the air. You know?"

"What's your mind-set today, with the burden of saving Pebble Beach on your shoulders?"

Kevin smiled again. "As the cliché goes, 'Play one shot at a time, and do the best I can.'"

"Were you the one who released the agreement to the press?"

"No."

"Who did?"

"Perhaps Mr. Leonard can help you with that one," Kevin said. "He was there when it was signed. He knew about the proposed sale before I did." Kevin glanced at Leonard, who was glaring at him. "Sorry, folks, but that's all I have time for."

He stepped away from the lectern and wove his way through the crowd, ignoring the questions that were being yelled at him. Ten minutes later he and Willie were on the practice range.

A temporary fence protected them from the huge crowd that had been awaiting their arrival. Kevin had been greeted with cheers. Usually, the fans that hang around the practice area are more knowledgeable about golf, as interested in a player's swing as in his or her score, and as quiet as spectators gathered around a green when a player is putting.

Not this day, though. Even after the cheering died down there was a constant hum of voices. Kevin sensed an excitement and electricity in the air that he had never experienced before. He tried not to let it affect him.

A minute after they'd arrived, a courtesy car drove up and Kaori Noro stepped out to more than a few boos. He smiled and bowed to the crowd before walking over to Kevin, who was practicing short shots with his lob wedge.

"Grandfather for caddie?" Noro asked. "That is good. My grandmother was caddie for many years. But grandmother or grandfather, *player* must still hit shots. It is difficult to do on Sunday afternoon. *Very* difficult during last Sunday afternoon ever for tournament at Pebble Beach." He started to walk away, then stopped and put both hands around his throat. "Very difficult to swallow."

Kevin skulled the next two wedge shots.

"Remember the metronome, lad," Willie said.

"Right."

It took a dozen balls for Kevin to calm down after Noro's pantomime. From that point on, though, he hit it pure.

He was ready for Pebble Beach.

CHAPTER 12

If Cypress Point is golf's "Sistine Chapel," Pebble Beach is the game's "Crown Jewel." In his prologue to the telecast of the AT&T tournament one year, CBS golf broadcaster Pat Sumerall painted a word picture of the course:

On the edge of a jagged Pacific Coastline lies a golf course that has no equal. It is revered as the ultimate playground, a blend of carpeted fairways, spectacular vistas, and the unending thunderous voice of the pounding surf.

Kevin left the practice tee to take on this Crown Jewel— and Kaori Noro. Hundreds of excited fans were standing around the putting green as he worked on pace and a smooth stroke. Many of the spectators also formed a narrow corridor to the first tee, and were packed 10-deep around it. He heard them calling his name as he walked to the tee; he tried to shut them out.

One voice got through, though. "Make me look good, Kevin!" It was Dr. Glouster, giving him a thumbs-up sign.

One other face came into focus. Sara was behind the tee,

peering over a man's shoulder. She gave him a hint of a smile and he returned it.

Noro came onto the tee dressed in white slacks, a white turtleneck and a red V-neck sweater. His bright red and white attire—a stark contrast to the conservative outfit of Kevin's and most of the other players—seemed to be meant to symbolize the flag of Japan, with its large red dot on a white background.

Kevin and Noro shook hands wordlessly. Kevin's strategy was not to let what Noro did on the golf course—good or bad—affect him. That might change over the last few holes— might cause him to be more aggressive or conservative—but he would deal with that if and when the time came. One thing he didn't have to deal with was the distraction of Larry Caldwell. They had missed the team cut by a single stroke.

Noro hit first, a perfect 3-wood into the center of the dog-leg on the 373-yard par 4. Trying not to push his drive into the trees as he had done on Friday, Kevin hung back on his right leg a fraction of a second. The gallery roared when the ball left the clubface, then groaned as it hooked out-of-bounds.

After hitting another tee-shot, Kevin recovered well and one-putted for a bogey. Noro parred the first hole, but eagled the second by holing an impossible bunker shot. Forgetting to play his own game, Kevin charged his birdie putt on the third green and missed the comebacker to go three down.

Noro and Kevin then matched pars until the seventh, the treacherous downhill par-3, which—at 107 yards—is the shortest hole on any championship golf course. On a calm day, most pros will hit a sand wedge. But the wind had increased fivefold as they reached the unprotected hilltop tee. Bordering the green and in back was the Pacific Ocean.

Kevin stood alone on the edge of the world and gazed down at the small, sand- and water-protected putting surface. He was debating between a 7- and 8-iron. Finally selecting the longer club, he hit a low shot that came to rest six feet from the flagstick. He then made the birdie putt to cut Noro's lead to two. It went back to three again when Noro holed a long chip on the eighth, and then to four after he hit a brilliant 6-iron to within three feet of the cup at No. 9.

The huge gallery, which had exploded when Kevin birdied the seventh, was now hushed. He was four strokes down with only nine holes to play. Shoulders visibly slumped, he stood on the 10th tee waiting for Noro to drive.

"One shot at a time, lad," Willie whispered. "I can assure you, he won't keep making birdies."

Kevin responded by holing a 30-foot putt on the 10th green for a birdie. It brought the deficit back to three and the fans back into the battle.

Providing something of a respite from the sea, the 11th turns inland toward 17-Mile Drive and the Del Monte Forest. Because the players in the group up ahead hadn't finished hitting their approach shots to the 384-yard par-4, Kevin had time to study the leader board. Kaori had a two-stroke lead over one player; Kevin was tied with two others for third.

When it was safe to tee-off, Kevin hit another good drive. But then—with a TV cameraman kneeling behind him and a nationwide audience watching—his adrenalin caused him to flush his approach and it flew into the bunker behind the green. After studying the lie, he anchored himself firmly in the sand. But then a photographer moved and it broke his concentration. He stepped out of the bunker, regrouped, reentered the sand, and then splashed the ball onto the green.

The gallery roared in approval when the ball rolled to within inches of the cup. Willie removed the flagstick, and Kevin tapped in his par putt.

Kevin was delayed in leaving the green by the swarm of spectators following the final twosome. When he got to the par-3 12th, he was surprised to see that Noro had already teed his ball.

Like Kevin, Kaori had made a par at the 11th hole. But Kevin had the honor because of his birdie at the 10th. Noro was in a discussion with his caddie, presumably deciding which club to use. Kevin said, "Excuse me, Kaori, but I believe I still have the tee." He smiled to show that there wasn't any gamesmanship involved.

Noro looked at Kevin and began shaking his head. "My honor. You just make six."

"No, Kaori, I had a four."

"Was six."

"Two in the bunker," Kevin said slowly, "out in three, one-putt. That's four."

"Two penalty strokes."

Kevin gaped at the Japanese player as a murmur moved through the crowd of spectators. "*Penalty?* For what?"

"Rule thirteen," Noro replied. "Testing sand."

"I didn't test the sand."

"In bunker, out of bunker, back in bunker. Test sand first time in." Noro yanked a club out of his bag as if to say there was nothing else to discuss.

"There's no rule against that unless I take a *different* stance," Kevin said. "I had a four."

"Sign for four, disqualified."

Kevin noticed a member of the Tour Staff walking onto the

:ee. "What's the problem?" Gil Maxwell asked.

"He claims I tested the sand on the last hole. I took my :tance, but then stepped out of the bunker because some photographer bothered me. I went back in, took the same :tance and then played the shot. No way did I test the sand."

Maxwell looked at Noro, who was shaking his head. "He :ested sand. Rule thirteen."

"I wasn't there, Kaori," Maxwell said. "But I'll have some-)ne review the tape in the TV trailer. Go ahead and keep playing and I'll give you a ruling as soon as I can."

The two golfers glared at each other. Now that he had made his point, Kevin stepped back and motioned for Noro :o hit. It would allow Kevin a few moments to calm down.

But the Japanese star, obviously wanting the same advan-:age, said, "You so anxious, I give you my turn."

For Kevin it was a no-win situation. Insist that Noro hit and it might appear that he was admitting to the penalty. Hit first, and Noro would have more time to regain his focus.

Kevin hit first, so angry that it was a miracle he made solid :ontact. Not so much due to a miracle, actually, but to Willie's gnarled finger moving back and forth, slowly and ,moothly, before Kevin swung the 2-iron and found the cen-er of the green. When Noro hit, his ball seemed headed for he front bunker but it carried onto the green. Both players :wo-putted for a three.

Maxwell approached them as they left the green. Kevin 'egarded him with dread. To go five strokes down now...

"There was no violation, Kaori. Kevin took the same :tance both times."

He took his stance in the bunker on 13, too, feathering the)all out of the sand with a lazy-looking swing, which belied the grim intensity seething within him. His landing target was six inches onto the green. That's where the Titleist hit rolling until it brushed the flagstick and fell into the hole. When Noro bogeyed, what was once a four-stroke lead had been reduced to one.

The 14th hole was the one behind Ted Osborne's mansion. After each player found the fairway on the 565-yard par-5, Noro laid up with a 4-iron to about 100 yards from the green. His turn to hit, Kevin pulled the cover off his 3-wood.

"Are you sure, lad?" Willie asked.

Kevin nodded and looked ahead toward the green. The wind was blowing hard behind him, but it was still a risky shot because of the out-of-bounds left and right. Without wasting time, Kevin made a good swing and launched the ball toward the left of the green. It ended up in the rough some 35 yards short of the putting surface. From there, Kevin would have the uphill pitch that Ted Osborne said he would have—and a good chance to get it close to the cup.

As Ted had also predicted, Noro's wind-carried wedge shot landed with little backspin and the ball rolled off the rear of the green. Because of where the flagstick was located—near a severe slope that dropped down to the green's lower level—Noro would be foolish to make an aggressive chip for birdie. He would probably have to settle for par. Sensing this, Kevin hit a delicate flop shot that stopped three feet to the left of the hole. He watched Noro make a sensational shot for a tap-in par, then rolled in the birdie putt to pull even.

Kevin was only vaguely aware of the fans urging him on. His anger at Noro's penalty ploy had been transformed into concentration so intense that it accepted only those factors required for proper execution of the shot at hand. Every other thought was rejected.

On the tee of the 15th hole, however, immediately after Kevin hit a drive that bisected the fairway, an outside element did manage to penetrate his trance. At impact, he felt a sting in his right thumb. Completing his swing, he turned his head and looked at it.

There were traces of red on the white bandage.

Mesmerized, he continued to stare at the bandage. Noro's supporters might have thought he was posing, holding the follow-through because he was so proud of the drive. They were wrong. Kevin came out of the follow-through finally and gave the driver to Willie.

"What is it, lad?"

Kevin showed him the bloodstained bandage.

"Can you swing?"

"I think so. That was the first time I felt it all day."

They heard a commotion in the crowd behind him. A marshal said, "Sir, please hold your position."

"I'm a doctor," Bill Glouster replied. He was trying to make his way to the tee.

"Let him through, please," Kevin said.

Glouster reached for Kevin's hand and looked at the bandage. "Does it hurt?"

"Just started. How bad is it?"

"Can't tell until I see the cut. In any case, you need a new dressing."

"Can you do it out here?"

"Sure," Glouster said. "I just need a few things. You still got that Motrin?"

"In my bag."

"Take a couple. I'll be back in a few minutes." He ducked

under the gallery rope and began squeezing through the crowd.

Kevin turned around and looked at Noro, who was waiting to hit his tee-shot. He had a scowl on his face.

"Sorry about the noise," Kevin said. "Please go ahead."

Still scowling, Noro hit his best drive of the day. The ball stopped rolling about 10 yards beyond Kevin's.

After laying down his bag, Willie got a bottle of water from a cooler at the back of the tee. Kevin swallowed two pills, then wrapped a white towel around his right hand. He was walking off the tee when Gil Maxwell joined him.

"The stitches came loose," Kevin told him. "The doctor who did the suturing went to get something to fix it. Okay?"

"Let me look at it."

Kevin unwrapped the towel. The bandage was almost all red.

"Yeah, you're gonna have to do something," Maxwell said.

"No penalty for getting this fixed, right?"

"No. Of course, we can't delay play forever. With that storm coming in, and with getting started late this morning, I was already worried about darkness. Tell your doctor to do his thing, but to do it as quickly as possible."

Noro was walking across the fairway toward them. "What now?" he demanded.

"The stitches on Kevin's thumb pulled loose. A doctor is getting something to fix it."

"For little cut, need doctor?"

"It's not so little, Kaori. It's bleeding pretty good."

Noro snickered at Kevin. "Need cart next? For you and grandfather?" He snickered again, then veered off and headed for his ball.

Kevin reached his own drive and waited while Willie determined the distance to the green. He stared at Noro for several seconds, wondering if he had anything to do with the razor blade on the door handle of the Riviera. The highly emotional gallery, which had reacted enthusiastically to almost every one of his shots, was now strangely hushed—just as they had been after Noro's birdies at eight and nine.

Since checking the scores on the 11th tee, Kevin had avoided looking at leader boards. He strolled over to the scorer assigned to their twosome. "Do you know how the rest of the field is doing?"

"You and Mr. Noro have a two-shot lead at nine under," she said.

Kevin thanked her and walked back to his golf ball.

"You have 100 yards to the front of the green," Willie said, returning his yardage book to his back pocket, "126 to the hole."

Kevin nodded. He was grateful to get his mind back where it belonged. "I would think the wind will knock it down some."

"A half-club more than normal, perhaps," Willie suggested. "Punch 8-iron."

"Sounds good." Kevin took the club out of the bag, made a couple of practice swings and tried to find the tempo that was so necessary for playing in the wind.

"Hold on, lad," Willie said. "The doctor's coming."

Kevin handed the iron to Willie and waited for the approaching cart. In a matter of seconds, Bill Glouster was snipping off the bloodstained bandage. Underneath was a gory mess.

"Jeeze," Kevin said. "Is it as bad as it looks?"

"We have to clean it up a little first."

Kevin flinched as Glouster cleaned the cut, then immediately felt embarrassed by it. He wondered what the TV announcers were saying at that moment; whether they were being derisive as Noro had been, or sympathetic and understanding.

"It looks like you only lost a couple of stitches," Dr. Glouster said. "Considering the pressure you've been putting on it, that's pretty good." In less than a minute, he had pulled the skin together and taped it and was applying a new bandage. "I made the dressing as thin as I could without sacrificing protection." The last piece of tape was snipped off. "It isn't perfect, but it should last four holes."

"Thanks, Bill," Kevin said. He pulled the 8-iron out of his bag and gripped it gingerly.

"How does it feel?"

"Tender."

"You take some Motrin?"

"Yeah."

"That should help soon," Glouster said, climbing back into the cart. "Mind over matter, Kevin. And if that doesn't work, try 'no pain, no gain.'" He smiled before he drove off.

As he had on the practice tee the day before, Kevin took a practice swing with hardly any pressure on the thumb. No problem. He took three more swings, gripping a little tighter each time, but felt only slight discomfort. He wouldn't allow himself to think of it as pain, and it didn't seem to be getting worse. The bandage remained white.

Ready to go finally, Kevin concentrated on making a low follow-through to keep the ball below the worst of the wind. But either he flinched or inadvertently favored the thumb, because he got his hands too far ahead at impact—just enough to push the ball to the right edge of the green. The flagstick, unfortunately, was way to the left. Kevin exchanged the 8-iron for his putter, watched Noro drill what looked like a 9-iron close to the hole, and walked halfway to the green before daring to look at the bandage. It was still white. But only after he had two-putted for par and Glouster's emergency repair job remained spotless did Kevin decide the bandage would last the round. Now all he had to worry about was Noro, who calmly stroked in the birdie putt for a one-stroke lead.

The final three holes would be match play—just as the first 15 had basically been, despite Kevin's mind-set to play the course and not Noro.

On the 16th tee, after Noro had hit only an average drive, Kevin opened his stance and produced a power fade that followed the par-4's right-turning fairway. It was a big drive, and it left him with only a pitching wedge approach over a grassy ditch that guarded the entrance to the green. With the cup cut just 12 feet from the back of the oval putting surface—which slanted from back-to-front and from right-to-left—anything over the green would be disastrous. Still, he felt he had to go for it. Noro was on but not close. Knowing that the next hole was playing into the wind, Kevin's chances of making birdie there were slim. He needed one now.

Kevin felt raindrops on his neck as he prepared to hit the wedge. It disrupted his concentration; he stepped away from the ball and started his preshot routine for a second time. But once again he stopped, this time looking at Willie for an answer to whatever it was that was troubling his mind.

"We don't want too much spin here," Willie said. "A small 9-iron, perhaps?"

They were teaming perfectly. A full wedge might land a little short and spin back off the green. Feeling more confident with the 9-iron in his hands, Kevin punched it onto the front of the well-sloped green and watched it begin to roll. The partisan fans, quieted by Noro's birdie at the previous hole, erupted as the ball hit and continued to cheer as it trickled down to a stop well within Kaori's own approach shot. It finished rolling four feet to the right of the cup.

"Well done, lad."

"I know that putt," Kevin said. "I can make it."

"Aye, that you can."

The Japanese star's putt was much longer and too dangerous to do anything more than lag it. Indicative of his much-admired short game, he did it beautifully. After Noro had tapped in his six-incher for par, Kevin replaced his ball and then crouched 10 feet behind it to look for the line. He saw it clearly, as if there was a track on the green that showed the right-to-left break into the hole. Sensing that the crowd around the green was holding its collective breath as he bent over the putt that would tie him again with Noro, Kevin had the strange sensation that he was the least nervous of all. Somehow, for some unexplainable reason, he knew the ball was going in.

No magical cocoon protected him as it had a few holes earlier; he was fully aware of what was going on—the fans, the photographers, the TV cameras. What was odd was that something miraculous in his brain was allowing him to feed off the drama. But instead of scaring him, it filled him with confidence. He took the putter blade back smoothly, and stroked the birdie putt into the center of the cup.

The roar that came from the crowd was deafening. Kevin looked at Willie and raised his eyebrows. His caddie nodded his approval, as much in appreciation for Kevin's calmness as for the stroke itself.

Even with the sheriff's deputies and marshals leading the

way through the mass of spectators, it took Kevin and Willie several minutes to reach the 17th tee. When they arrived, Kevin noticed that the wind had abated somewhat. *The lull before the storm?* No doubt. The sky had turned gray and the ocean in the distance looked angry.

Kevin stood staring at the green that sat some 200 yards away. It was shaped like the number 8 lying on its side. Like the 16th at Cypress, the 17th at Pebble was a famous hole. It was where Jack Nicklaus had hit the flagstick to secure his 1972 U.S. Open championship, and where Tom Watson had deprived the "Golden Bear" of the same title a decade later, chipping in for a birdie that nailed down his only Open victory. The thought caused Kevin to glance at the pocket of his golf bag that held the Watson glove.

Fingering the sole of his 2-iron, Kevin looked at Willie and got a nod in return. He pulled out the club and gripped it lightly. The flagstick, set in its traditional Sunday placement, was located on the left side of the green behind a gaping bunker. Kevin took a brief look at the bandage on his right hand, made only a partial practice swing, and then set up to his ball. Moments later, the Titleist was flying toward the target. Drawing slightly, the ball skirted the right edge of the sand, landed nine feet short of the cup and rolled that same distance beyond it.

The pressure was on Noro now, and the fans around the tee knew it. Would he finally crack? Only an hour ago he had been cruising along with a three-stroke lead. Now he was tied, his opponent within birdie range. When the cheering for Kevin's shot finally stopped, he showed why he was the world's top player: his tee-shot landed on the green and came to rest one foot inside of Kevin's.

Walking to the green, Kevin tried to maintain the positive attitude he'd had on the previous putt. In golf, he knew—possibly more than in any other sport—positive thoughts could disappear in seconds. Looking over his birdie putt, he wondered if his were still there. Something else Kevin knew was that the cup would appear smaller for Noro if he holed his putt first. No, not if...*when* he made his putt first.

It was a downhill putt, so he didn't dare charge it and risk having a four-footer coming back. *That* would not be good on his nerves. Yet it was these very same nerves that betrayed him as the putter made contact. The jabbed ball darted forward and clearly would have gone more than four feet beyond the hole if it hadn't hit the back of the cup and jumped two inches into the air—as if taking a bow—before falling straight down and disappearing.

From the frenzied gallery came a thunder that had to have rattled the windows in downtown Carmel. Kevin shook his head in wonder; the gods of golf had finally given him one.

Being the tough competitor that he was, Noro made a much smoother stroke. When the ball was a foot from the hole, it appeared to onlookers that it couldn't miss. Noro raised his putter in triumph and stepped toward the cup. Then suddenly he stopped—mouth dropping open in disbelief—as the ball hit something. Perhaps it was a spike mark or a large grain of sand that caused it to bounce, and a bouncing putt is seldom true. Catching only the right lip of the cup, the ball cruelly spun out. Noro stared at the offending sphere for several seconds, finally backhanding it into the hole for his par.

Kevin Courtney was leading the tournament by one stroke...with one hole to go.

In all of golf, no hole is more picturesque than the 545-yard

18th at Pebble Beach. Both the "Beauty" and the "Beast," it is arguably the world's most famous finishing hole. Even under calm conditions, with only a five-dollar bet on the line, it tests the ability and nerves of all players. When the wind is howling, however, and the waves are crashing on the rocky beach that borders the left side of the hole, it is the ultimate examination of a golfer's skill and courage.

Well aware that he had birdied five of the last eight holes, a par was all that Kevin was thinking about as he prepared to hit his drive. The deteriorating conditions made it highly unlikely that Noro would make the birdie that he needed. If he somehow did, Kevin's par would still ensure a tie. Kevin envisioned a safe tee-shot that avoided the out-of-bounds stakes to the right, a conservative second shot, a careful approach to the center of the green, and two putts.

Willie pulled the 1-iron out of the bag. Kevin dried his hands on a towel, made sure the grip was dry as well, then stepped out from under the umbrella that Willie was holding above their heads. He hit the shot pure, and with a slight cut. It bore through the wind, curved away from the ocean and rolled to a stop just inside the right rough. Kevin tried to gauge the ball's position in relation to the large tree that guarded that side of the hole. He looked at Willie and mouthed "Blocked?" His caddie shrugged and shook his head, unable to reassure him due to the rain and gathering darkness. It was only when they were almost to the Titleist— after Noro had pushed his drive nearly out-of-bounds—that they saw that Kevin had a clear line to the green.

Two more good swings, Kevin thought. *Just like the one you just made.*

While he waited for Noro to hit his layup shot from the deep rough, Kevin toweled off the grip of his 5-iron. He knew Willie had already tended to it, but he did it anyway. He then dried his right hand, careful not to loosen the bandage. Finally, it was his turn to hit. His last thought, just as he began his downswing, was that he wished to God that the shot was successfully over with.

It wasn't a wet grip or a wet hand or a sore thumb that caused him to come over the top on his downswing and yank the ball left—toward the angry ocean. It was because of the same pressure which ultimately had forced him off the tour. Because of the darkness, he couldn't see the ball go over the edge. But he knew that it had, probably close to 150 yards short of the green. The startled gasp from the crowd told him so, too. He trudged toward the jagged coastline, the wind tearing at him with increasing ferocity the closer he got to the water. Momentarily, he thought of the millions of shocked viewers who were watching on television. What were they thinking? What were they saying? What names were they making up at that very moment for Kevin Courtney?

If the officials and marshals had been successful in finding the ball on the rocks or the beach below, Kevin might have tried a one-in-a-million attempt to get it back into play. But the second he hit it, he knew the ball was lost. Everything was lost. Gil Maxwell determined where the ball had last crossed the hazard and indicated to Kevin where to drop another Titleist. He was too chagrined to even make eye contact with the Tour Official, and just nodded quietly. Then, once the new ball was in play, he paced impatiently as Willie dried the grip of his 8-iron.

"Think a moment, lad," Willie said, "while I get you a new glove."

Kevin shook his head.

"You can still beat him, Kevin," his caddie said firmly.

Kevin. He looked hard at Willie before stepping under the umbrella. He pulled off the wet glove, dried his hands and put on the new one that Willie had retrieved from his bag.

"Let's get our six and move on, lad. Noro has little chance of making birdie."

Kevin saw Willie's finger move back and forth like a metronome, then went into his preshot routine. Swinging smoothly, he watched his ball pierce the rain and ever-blackening sky and finish in the middle of the green. With the penalty stroke, he now lay four. It was all up to Noro. Surprisingly, though, the world's best player left his 15-foot birdie putt about five inches short—dead in the heart of the cup. After Kevin had two-putted for his six, both players were 10 under par, one stroke ahead of their nearest competitor.

The next day, there would be a sudden-death playoff for the championship...and for Pebble Beach.

CHAPTER 13

In golf—professional and amateur alike—it's traditional for playing companions to shake hands at the completion of a round. Kevin and Noro ignored this tradition and simply stared at each other from a distance. Grinning suddenly, Kaori reached up and clutched his throat with his right hand, a message not lost on Kevin or any of the hundreds of drenched spectators who were watching. Some had applauded when Kevin holed his bogey putt; the only real cheering came when Noro's birdie attempt stopped short.

Kevin knew he didn't deserve cheers—not even polite applause. He *had* choked. Everyone should have been celebrating and congratulating him, maybe even carrying him off on their shoulders for saving Pebble Beach. But instead, he felt shame and embarrassment. He wondered again what the announcers on television were saying. Wondered if some people were embarrassed for him. Wondered if Joey would be embarrassed, too. Eyes averted, he left Willie with the bag and entered the scoring tent.

His clothing was soaked. He had walked up the fairway in a daze. No hat, no rain pants, his jacket askew enough that the rain ran down his back. After the nightmarish second shot, nothing else had mattered.

Shivering, Kevin sat at a table near Noro and forced himself to concentrate on confirming his hole-by-hole numbers on the scorecard. Bile burned in his throat as he stared at his 6 on the 18th hole. Delaying the inevitable no longer, he swallowed and signed the card.

Gil Maxwell was waiting for them outside the tent. "Obviously, gentlemen, you can't play off in the dark. We'll start on the 15th hole tomorrow morning at nine o'clock. Any questions?"

"Request Rules Official there," Kaori said.

Kevin glanced at him, then looked away.

"Don't worry, standard procedure," Maxwell said. "Everybody's waiting for you guys in the Media Center. I'll see you tomorrow."

Maxwell was wrong: not everybody was in the Media Center. A man with a CBS logo on his nylon jacket grabbed Kevin's arm as Maxwell walked away. "Come with me."

Kevin resisted the man's hand and stood staring at him. "That's a good way to lose that hand, Bud."

The CBS man released his grip. "It will only take..."

"Get lost," Kevin told him. When he felt someone grab his other arm, he angrily started to pull free. It was Dr. Glouster.

"Whoa, we need to look at that thumb, Kevin," he said.

Before Kevin could respond, another Tour official confronted him. "Media Center, please. Mr. Noro is already on the way."

"I'm due for my shift at the hospital," Glouster said to

Kevin. "We could do it here now, or you can drive all the way out there later."

"More stitches?"

"Probably."

Kevin nodded. He glanced over the sea of faces for Sara but didn't see her. "Let's go to my office in the pro shop."

"But the media..." the Tour official stammered.

"I'll be there soon," Kevin said. "C'mon, Bill."

The deputies and marshals were waiting as Kevin, Glouster, and Willie left the area of the 18th green and headed for the pro shop. It was still raining, although not as hard, and many spectators had left or gone inside one of the nearby buildings. Quite a few had remained, though, and they called to Kevin as he walked past.

"Get him tomorrow in the playoff, Kevin!" a woman yelled.

Tomorrow? Play-off? He had vaguely heard what Gil Maxwell had said about that. Suddenly it hit him: the playing of a single hole tomorrow could determine the future of Pebble Beach, as well his own future. One hole, maybe one shot. He shivered noticeably.

"You could use a hot shower," Glouster said.

"I'll be all right."

Willie was walking ahead of them, Kevin's large, Titleist staff bag slung over his right shoulder. *He's got to be as wet as I am,* Kevin thought. *And just as cold. He should be home in front of his fireplace, not out here.*

They arrived at the pro shop, pushed through another crowd of customers, and finally reached the security of Kevin's office. "I need a dry towel for these clubs, lad," Willie said.

"Just leave the bag there and one of my staff will take care of it. You need to get home and get into some dry clothes. I'll have someone drive you."

Willie started to object but Kevin stopped him. "We'll take care of your bike and pick you up in the morning."

Willie shook his head. "Thank you, but I want to ride."

"Willie, that's ridiculous. It's miserable out and you're soaked."

"'Tis the weather of Scotland," Willie replied with a smile. "And I have ridden in it for many, many years. However, if someone would be so kind as to look after the clubs, I will leave now. What time in the morning?"

"It's really not a problem to..."

"Lad?"

Kevin sighed. "Seven-thirty. If you decide that you want a ride, call the pro shop. Okay? And be careful."

"I will," Willie said.

After he'd left, Glouster said, "Tough old guy. But you, Kevin, don't have that Scottish blood. All the clothes in there," he said, indicating the pro shop, "you must have something you can change into."

"Aren't you in a hurry to get to the hospital?"

"Yeah, and you'll be there, too—with pneumonia. I can wait."

Five minutes later, Kevin was sitting at his desk in dry clothes and with his right hand resting palm-up on the flat surface.

"If it's okay with you," Glouster said, "I won't take time for an anaesthetic. I'll barely penetrate the skin; it'll feel like pinpricks."

Kevin looked up at him. "Let me ask you something, Bill. Ever screw up and lose a patient?"

Glouster's eyes told Kevin that he knew that that really wasn't the question. "Weather like this, anybody could have bogeyed 18. Even Nicklaus. Good God, Kevin, you shot 32 on the back nine."

"Big deal," Kevin said. "I needed 31."

Glouster reached into his equipment bag and brought out a needle forceps with triple-zero suture attached. In minutes, he had closed the wound with four tiny sutures and bandaged the thumb.

Kevin inspected the work. "I can't thank you enough, Bill. When this is over—if there's still a Pebble Beach Golf Links—I'd like you to be my guest for a round."

"I accept," Glouster said quickly. "Pebble is still going to be here, Kevin. You're better than Noro. That 32 proved it, so don't let one shot get you down." He closed his bag, started for the door then stopped. "Hell, man, we're all human. You know?"

Glouster hadn't answered Kevin's question about screwing up, and he had tried to blame the bogey on 18 on the weather. His last three words, though, said otherwise: "We're all human."

Being human, Noro had parred 18. Being human, Kevin had bogeyed it. Thanks to Willie, he hadn't *double*-bogeyed it. He still had a chance. A knock on the door interrupted his thoughts. When he opened it, Masaru Komoto was standing on the other side.

"May I have a word?"

Kevin motioned him inside, then closed the door again.

"I am aware that the ladies and gentlemen of the media are awaiting you," Komoto said. "Before you meet them, I would like to dispose of a misconception that you may have about our agreement."

"Misconception?" Kevin asked.

"To win our little wager, you had to defeat Kaori Noro. Correct?"

"Yes."

"You failed to do that today."

"I didn't do it yesterday, either," Kevin said, "or Thursday or Friday. But that doesn't have anything to do with our agreement. It's the total score that counts."

"You and Kaori are now tied," Komoto said patiently. "Correct?"

"Yeah, so?"

"Let us assume that another player finished ahead of both of you. The tournament would be over. Do you agree that you would have lost our wager?"

Kevin shook his head. "You know what, Komoto? I'm too tired to play games with you. Last night you said you were a man of integrity. What other lies did you tell me?"

"No lies, young man. But I must confess that I misjudged your courage the night we made our wager. I want you to know that I am prepared to pay the consequences, should there be any." His countenance softened. "I feared that there might be a question by the media concerning our agreement. *Technically*—as you Americans say—it could be argued that a tie for the lead after four rounds constitutes your losing. Technically, you didn't beat him. *Technically*, therefore, you lost." He paused. "Let it not be so. Should you win tomorrow, Pebble Beach remains as it is. I am a man of my word." After bowing slightly, and receiving a nod from Kevin, Komoto left.

Kevin assumed Noro would long be finished by the time he reached the interview room. The Japanese star, however, was still sitting before the media. There was an empty chair on the other side of Noro and Richard Gardner. Kevin squared his shoulders, stepped onto the podium and sat down.

"Kaori has already gone over his round, Kevin," Gardner said. "You can do that, too, after he leaves. But I believe there are some questions for the two of you."

"Kevin, tell us about the dispute on 11," a reporter asked.

Kevin shrugged. "He thought I incurred a penalty. Gil Maxwell disagreed."

Noro shook his head. "In bunker, out of bunker, back in bunker. Testing sand. Two-stroke penalty. Tournament should be over."

Kevin shrugged again, as if to say 'The guy won't take no for an answer.'

"What happened to your thumb out there, Kevin?"

"Some stitches pulled loose when I hit my drive on 15. Luckily, the doctor who had stitched it up the first time was in the gallery."

Noro began shaking his head again. "Delay of play. More penalty strokes."

"Tell us about 18, Kevin."

Kevin looked at Gardner. "I thought you said 'both of us.'"

"Here's one for both of you," a voice called out. "Why didn't you shake hands following the round?"

Noro shrugged his shoulders but said nothing. Kevin started to do the same, then remembered Noro's "choke" gesture on the 18th green. "I had no reason to shake his hand."

"Meaning what?"

"Just what I said."

"If you win tomorrow, Kaori, in a sense, you will be destroying Pebble Beach. Does that bother you?"

The Japanese star nodded his head sideways toward Kevin. "Destroy it today with bogey on 18. He have his chance. Blew it."

Kevin looked at him tight-lipped. Richard Gardner said, "All right, Kaori, thanks for your time. We'll let you go now." Noro laughed, stood up, glanced at Kevin, then swaggered from the packed room.

Kevin began reviewing his round for the reporters and writers. There were few questions until he got to the final hole.

"So what happened on your second shot?"

There were several excuses he could have used—his thumb, a slippery grip, the wet glove—but he didn't. But he also couldn't publicly acknowledge that he had choked. "I made a bad swing. Maybe it was the pressure. I'm not sure."

As usual, Dean Adams was in the front row. "What does this mean, Courtney?" He clutched his hands to his throat.

"Ask Noro."

"I think," Adams said, smirking, "that he was telling you that you choked. What do *you* think?"

"I think," Kevin replied, "that you're not as dumb as you look."

It got a laugh. Adams's face turned red.

Someone asked him about his strategy for the playoff the next day.

"It's kind of a paradox. Four days of stroke play, now it's basically match play. Hard to know how either one of us will handle it."

"Why so much animosity between the two of you?"

Kevin was thoughtful for a few moments, then leaned forward in his chair. "I don't know if you'd call it 'animosity.' He wrote down a six for my score on 11 instead of the four that I said I had. That doesn't exactly make me want to join the Kaori Noro fan club."

"But he thought you had incurred a penalty for testing the

sand."

"Even if I had, his job is to write down the score I tell him. If that score is proved to be wrong and I sign for it, then I will be penalized. He has no right to tell *me* what my score is. My score is what I tell *him*. If he wants to protest it after the round, that's his business. He has every right to. But I'll tell you this," Kevin said, "most players that I have played with on the Tour would never have done what he did. If they thought I'd incurred a penalty, and it was clear that I didn't realize it because I didn't add any extra strokes to the score I thought I had, they would've pulled me aside and quietly pointed it out. That's the gentlemanly way to do it." He sat back in his chair.

"Kevin, how did you feel after that bogey on 18?"

It was the question he had been waiting for, the one he knew he couldn't answer because he wasn't inclined to bare his soul that completely—especially to the media. He smiled. "As my old grandmother in Indiana used to say, 'Pretty poorly.' But, thankfully, I have a chance to make up for it tomorrow. Sorry, guys, but it's been a long day. I gotta get out of here."

More questions were shouted as he walked to the door, and reporters and TV crews followed him down the stairs. The two deputies and his assistant, Jerry, were waiting at the bottom. Kevin could tell by the look on Jerry's face that something was wrong. Jerry started to speak, but Kevin stopped him. Whatever it was, the media didn't need to know.

"Let's go to my office."

The pro shop wasn't quite as crowded as it had been earlier. Kevin was actually surprised that it was even open. Several customers asked for his autograph but he declined by holding up his bandaged thumb to indicate that he couldn't write. All he wanted to do was find out what Jerry seemed so worried about. They went into his office and closed the door.

"What wrong?"

"I hate to tell you this, Kevin," Jerry said, "but a little while ago, Willie was struck by a hit-and-run driver."

Kevin stared at him in disbelief. "Oh my God. How bad?"

"Not sure yet. He was unconscious when they took him to the hospital."

Kevin sank into the chair behind his desk. "What happened?"

"All I know is that some jogger found him next to the road outside Pacific Grove."

"Jesus," Kevin said. "Why the hell did I let him ride that damned bike?" He shook his head. "Are you sure it's him?"

Jerry nodded. "Yep. One of the cart staff was driving by and saw him being put into the ambulance. He saw Willie with your bag this morning and wished him luck. He called me when he got home."

Kevin stood up. "I'm going to go to the hospital."

"Anything you want me to do?"

"Try to keep it to yourself until I can find out something, I guess," Kevin said. "Once Dean Adams hears about it, he'll probably blame *this* on me, too."

Five minutes later, Kevin was on 17-Mile Drive heading for the hospital. Due to the darkness and the wet highway, the traffic was agonizingly slow. *A hit-and-run driver*, Kevin thought. Then: *Or…could it have been the same person who bribed the kid and put the razor blade on my door handle?* He suddenly noticed that his speed had increased. He slowed down.

Could someone want me to lose so badly that they would willing to hurt or kill an innocent man? It was hard to imagine.

Kevin's fingers tightened around the steering wheel as he

pulled into the Emergency Room entrance. Was it someone who worked for Komoto? Someone Kevin didn't know about who would definitely be hurt financially if the development didn't go through? Was Jack Leonard somehow involved? If so, why? He'd lose his job if Pebble Beach were developed. Why would he want that? Or was it someone else?

Kevin parked the car and ran into the hospital. Amazingly, the first person he saw was Dr. Glouster. "We have to stop meeting like this," Glouster deadpanned.

"How's Willie?" Kevin blurted. "Is he okay?"

"Relax, Kevin," the doctor said, "he's fine. He's awake and alert and his vitals are good. C'mon, I'll take you to him."

Willie was lying on a table in the treatment room with his eyes closed. Kevin thought he looked dead. But when he touched his hand, Willie opened his eyes. "And a good evening to you, lad."

Kevin smiled at the greeting. "How're you feeling, my friend?"

"Like a car just ran over me," Willie said. There was a purple bruise in the center of his forehead. "Or was it a truck? My eyesight isn't so good lately." He grinned.

"Yeah, well," Kevin said, "as long as you don't give me a 6-iron when I need a 9, there shouldn't be a problem."

"The doctor here says I won't be looping for you tomorrow, lad."

Kevin looked at Glouster. "His right ankle is either broken or badly sprained. We'll know after we get him to X-ray."

"What about the bruise?"

"Possibly a slight concussion."

Kevin looked down at Willie again and shook his head. "You and that bike."

"Yes, I know: I should have listened to you," Willie said. He moved slightly and sucked in his breath before giving Kevin a wry smile. "Sometimes my Scotch stubbornness gets me in a wee bit of trouble."

No, Kevin thought, *it was my stupidity in thinking that I could save Pebble Beach. That's what caused all of this.*

"Willie, does your bike have reflectors on it?"

"Aye. Three big ones."

"Could you maybe have accidentally pulled in front of the car in the dark?"

"No. I always ride on the shoulder. You can get hurt ridin' your bike on the road."

Kevin and the doctor laughed. "I've heard that," Kevin said. He patted Willie's hand. "Anything I can do for you?"

"Win the tournament," Willie said. He lifted his hand and moved the index finger back and forth like a metronome.

CHAPTER 14

It was still raining when Kevin left the hospital and headed back to Pebble Beach for his ritualistic walk to the 18th tee. For once, he wondered why the hell he was going to do it. Did he really think that walking out there in miserable weather would somehow help him beat Noro the next day? Probably not. But then, he needed all the help he could get. *Jesus,* Kevin thought. *I don't have a caddie.*

He reached for his car phone and got Ted Osborne's number from Directory Assistance. Ted's teenaged son, Johnny, had once caddied for Kevin in a local tournament and had done an excellent job. Osborne answered on the second ring.

"Hi, Ted. It's Kevin Courtney. Is Johnny there?"

"No, he's next door, Kevin. Anything I can help you with?"

"My caddie had an accident tonight, so I need someone to lug my sticks around tomorrow morning. Think it'd hurt him to skip a day of school?"

"Not when you make all A's, Kevin. He'll be tickled to death. He really admires you."

"Could you have him meet me on the range about 7:30?"

"I'll deliver him personally," Osborne said. "Good luck, buddy. We're all pulling like hell for you."

Kevin thanked him and hung up the phone. *Yeah, I know everyone's pulling for me. That's one of my problems.*

The Riviera's headlights illuminated a street sign as Kevin drove past it. *Deer Lane.* It was Jack Leonard's street. What had Jerry told him that morning? That last night's storm had blown down a tree in front of Jack's garage? Kevin remembered seeing Jack's white Mercedes in its usual parking spot when he'd arrived for the final round. Since this was Sunday, there was probably no way they could have had that tree removed. If he was home, Jack's car would be in the driveway. Kevin slowed the Riviera as quickly as he could, pulled onto the shoulder, then turned around and went back.

He pulled past the Leonard's winding, tree-lined driveway and parked the car two houses down. The lawns were large in this neighborhood and the houses set quite a bit back from the road. What street lamps there were, were few and far between. Kevin figured the lack of light was to discourage tourists from driving through; burglars probably loved it. He took a flashlight from the car's console and put on a rain jacket that was on the back seat. Somewhere off to his left, a dog barked.

The redwood house sat some 70 yards from the road. The garage was on the left. Even during the daytime, most of both structures was hidden by trees and bushes. Kevin used the protection of the foliage as he started up the driveway.

Two windows were lit: the large one in front where the living room was located, and the one on the side of the house that looked out from Jack's den. Thanks to the light from the smaller window, Kevin could see Jack's car sitting well back from the front of the garage. Less than a minute later, he saw the fallen cypress tree. The dog barked again and Kevin looked in that direction. When he looked back, the light in the den was out. A stroke of luck? Or would he soon see Jack's face in the glass?

Kevin counted to 30 silently, then ran in a crouch to the driver's side of the car. Squatting to keep his head below the roofline, he cupped his left hand over the bulb end of the flashlight and flicked it on. He experimented with controlling the brightness for a moment, then scooted forward and inspected the left front fender. It was unmarked.

Because the hood was lower than the roof, Kevin knew he would have to crawl on his hands and knees to get around to the other side of the car. Feeling frightened and foolish at the same time, he counted to 30 again, took a quick glance at the house, then made his move. The rustle of his nylon jacket seemed extremely loud to his ears. He reached the right wheel-well, swung his body around, and rose to his knees. With his back to the den window now, he knew he could block at least some of the beam from the flashlight. When he turned it on, he saw the red paint.

The streak of color started just back of the headlight rim and appeared to be about six inches long. It was maybe a half-inch wide at the front end, but it thinned quickly. It reminded Kevin of the mark that a wooden tee sometimes made on the bottom of his driver. That, too, came from a glancing blow.

You son of a bitch.

Kevin turned off the flashlight, stood up and began walking down the driveway. He almost wished someone *would* see him and call the police. Seeing the look on Jack's face when he opened the front door to a couple of cops might be fun. But then Kevin thought of Willie's frequent admonition: "Don't rush it, lad."

It was difficult, but he waited until he had driven out of the neighborhood before he called 911.

"There was a hit-and-run accident earlier this evening near Pacific Grove," he told the dispatcher. "An elderly man on a bicycle. The car that hit him is at 7916 Deer Lane. It's a white Mercedes, and I think you'll find that the paint on the right fender matches a red Schwinn bike." He hung up.

When he arrived at the course, Kevin exchanged his wet loafers for the extra pair of golf shoes he always carried in his trunk. He also brought the flashlight with him.

The wind off Carmel Bay wasn't as strong on the 18th as it had been earlier in the day. Even though it was dark, Kevin could still determine the spot where he'd played that disastrous second shot. He'd remember it the next day, too—if the playoff got that far.

When he reached the tee, Kevin walked all the way to the back. He wondered whether the police would use their sirens when they went to check out the Mercedes. And if they did, whether he would hear it. He turned in the direction of Jack's house, and for what seemed to be the hundredth time that week, wondered *why*?

Jack had one of the most prestigious jobs in golf, and he lived in one of the most affluent and desirable localities in America. Why would anyone in that position want to destroy Pebble Beach? Had Komoto offered him an even better job, for even more money? Had he gotten into financial trouble from trying to keep up with his much more wealthy neighbors? Had he made some bad investments? Or was he just greedy? Kevin decided it was probably pure greed. Simple as that.

Suddenly, he couldn't wait to get home and get into the shower. He was shivering, and he couldn't tell if it was from the cold or from the craziness of the day. He needed a drink, too, and to call Sara. He took two steps forward, then stopped when he saw the large man standing 30 yards to his right.

In that unmistakable high-pitched voice of his, Jack Leonard said, "You really screwed things up for me, Kevin. You know that?"

"What are you talking about, Jack?"

Leonard laughed. "You're a lousy commando, you asshole. Ever hear of security systems? Sensors? Not all of them turn on a light in the yard. Some of them go off in the house. Mine beeps," Leonard said. "One beep, it's a small animal. Two beeps, it's something else. I knew who was checking out my car the moment I saw you." He began walking toward the tee, and that's when Kevin saw the gun in his hand.

"Move back where you were," Leonard said. "To the edge there. Maybe I'll find out why you like looking down on those rocks so much." He snickered. "Jesus, what a fucking dramatic asshole you are."

"Why would you try to kill Willie?" Kevin asked. He was walking backward, turning to look behind him as he went. He stopped a few feet from the edge. "You have the greatest job in the world. Why destroy Pebble Beach?"

"You don't have a clue, do you?"

"Apparently not."

"You think I'm happy with what I make when all these bastards around here live in multimillion dollar houses?"

"You have a wonderful home."

"It's a hovel," Leonard sneered.

"Who's paying you to do this? Komoto?"

Leonard was close enough that Kevin could see him smile. "We're paying *him*."

"I don't understand."

"Who do you think he's selling this place to? Another foreigner? No way we'd let that happen."

Kevin suddenly felt as if someone had punched him in the stomach. "You and *Joan*? My ex-wife's in on this?"

"Finally, the light goes on."

It was such an astounding thought that Kevin wanted to laugh. Only the sight of the gun stopped him. "You two don't have that kind of money," he said.

"No, but our syndicate does."

"Joan put this together, didn't she?"

"Hey, you're brighter than I thought," Leonard said. "Too bad that Joan's a lot brighter. Personally, I didn't think you had a chance to win the bet. She thought otherwise—even though she hates your guts for that little fling you had way back when."

"Did she bribe my caddie?" Kevin asked.

Leonard nodded. "The razor blade was her idea, too. I must say I'm impressed that you're still in it. But then, I also have to thank you for that stupid shot you hit on 18 today. If you hadn't gagged like that, I wouldn't have had a chance to keep this deal going. Wouldn't have had a chance to come up with a few ideas of my own."

"Jack, how can you be a part of destroying Pebble Beach?"

"Shit. All the money I'm going to make when this is over? I can buy my *own* golf course."

Just as Joey had said, the man who had come to the house

to see his mom was big. Kevin figured Jack would try to shove him onto the rocks below the tee. Lots of people knew Kevin visited the tee at night. They'd think he slipped on the wet grass in the dark. Some, of course, would also speculate that he had committed suicide because of the way he'd embarrassed himself on national television. The gun was just to get him into position; Jack was strong enough to kill someone without it.

Kevin felt the wooden rails of the low protective fence against the back of his legs. He then heard a siren in the distance. "Hear that, Jack?"

Leonard listened for a second. "So what?"

"They're on their way to your house," Kevin said. "I told them where to find the car that hit Willie."

"Bullshit. You didn't go in the pro shop; you came right out here. I watched you."

"Ever hear of a car phone, Jack. Nine, One, One?"

"You *dumb* ass," Leonard hissed. "You're ruining everything that we've worked so hard to put together."

"Listen to me, Jack," Kevin said. A gust of wind jarred them both. Leonard's hand appeared to tighten on the gun. "You might not have to go to jail for the hit-and-run, but you definitely will if you shoot me. An' once they hear that voice of yours, you'll be somebody's girlfriend in about a week. They'll come for you every night, Jack. Think about it."

A painful sound started from inside the big man and grew louder. He bared his teeth like a cornered bear. "We've...worked...so...hard...for this!" Suddenly, with a scream, he lunged toward Kevin. Anticipating it, Kevin had been secretly digging the cleats of his left golf shoe into the wet turf. When his attacker leaped at him, he pushed off to his right.

Leonard's heavy, hurtling body grazed Kevin's shoulder before it splintered the wooden rails like tooth picks. Falling to the ground from the blow, Kevin didn't see him go over the edge—but he heard it. A helpless, hopeless scream pierced the night.

Kevin lay there, heart pounding, too weak to stand. He felt more tired than he'd ever felt in his whole life. Unwilling to trust his coordination, he pulled the flashlight from his jacket pocket and crawled to the edge of the drop-off. Somehow, Jack had spun around in mid-air. He was lying on his back with his eyes open, his head and neck bent at an odd angle. Kevin threw up when he saw him.

He was shivering uncontrollably when he reached the Riviera. His right shoulder was aching from the fall to the ground and his head throbbed. He found six old aspirin in the bottom of the console and managed to get them down. It made him gag again. When he pulled out of the parking lot, the car's heater was on full blast.

No flashing blue lights were visible when he passed Deer Lane. Kevin wondered about Jo Leonard. Unless she was in on the whole thing, she was probably frightened that the police had come to talk to Jack about a hit-and-run accident. She would spend a sleepless night wondering if he could have done such a thing, and then—later—why he hadn't come home. In the morning, someone would inform her that her husband was dead.

Kevin considered calling 911 again, but didn't. Both the body and the car would be found soon enough, and the inevitable investigation would probably conclude that Jack had been so distraught about the hit-and-run that he'd killed himself at his beloved Pebble Beach. Accidentally slipped before he used the gun, or maybe just jumped.

Your plan worked, Jack, Kevin thought. *Wrong guy, though.*

Ten minutes later, at nearly 9:30 p.m., he was ringing the doorbell at the house where his son lived.

CHAPTER 15

When she opened the door, his ex-wife was clearly annoyed to see who it was. "It's late, Kevin. Joey's asleep."

"I figured he would be. I need to see *you*."

Joan looked at his wet hair, grass-stained slacks and golf shoes and shook her head. "What're you, drunk? Been rolling around in the rough with one of your little friends?"

"No, Joan," Kevin said quietly, "I'm not drunk. How 'bout we keep our voices down?"

She cocked her head. "Why? You afraid your son will find out what his father's really like? Better now than later, if you ask me."

"This won't take long."

"Forget it, you jerk!" She tried to close the door but Kevin held it open with his left arm and body.

"I know about your plan to buy Pebble Beach," Kevin said.

"Get out of my house!"

"Jack's dead, Joan."

Instantly, she stopped struggling and stared at him wide-eyed. Deep down—for Joey's sake—Kevin had hoped she wasn't involved. But now he knew. "Let's go inside and talk," he said. "Somewhere where there's no chance that Joey will hear us."

He followed her into the living room but remained standing when she sat down on one end of the couch. "I know everything, Joan," Kevin said. "You bribing my caddie, you putting the razor blade on my door handle. The bribery might not count for much, but the other one sounds like 'attempt to do bodily harm.'"

"We're divorced," Joan said defiantly but weakly. "Stuff like that happens all the time. A fine, maybe."

"If that was all, yeah," Kevin said. He started to slowly pace back and forth in front of his ex-wife. She watched him intently.

"Jack tried to kill my caddie tonight. Someone's going to jail for that, and it won't be him."

"I don't know anything about that, " Joan pleaded. "I swear to God, Kevin. If it happened, it was all Jack's idea. I don't know *anything* about it. Honest to God." She began to bite her lower lip.

A lie, or just fear? Kevin wasn't sure. "Accessory to attempted murder, Joan," he said.

Her shoulders slumped and she put her face in her hands for a moment. "I need a drink," she said. Abruptly, she got up and went into the kitchen. Kevin heard a cupboard door open, something make a "clunk" on the counter, and then glass against glass. She came back into the room with about two inches of whiskey. After drinking half of it, she looked up at Kevin. "What do you want?"

"This syndicate," he said. "Any of them in on your little

tricks?"

"No." She smiled wryly. "Everything was going so perfect. Then that *stupid* Komoto made the bet. We spent months putting this together." She shook her head sadly and sighed.

"Look," Kevin said. "Unless the police figure it out, and it's very possible that they will, I'm not going to say anything about what you've done."

She looked up at him, her eyes questioning. Finding an answer finally, she took another sip from her glass. "And in return, you get Joey. Right?"

"Only the joint custody that I should have had all along," Kevin replied. "Every other weekend and at least one night a week. If you and I agree that it won't be too hard for him or hurt his schoolwork, maybe a couple of nights. And half the time in the summer. You and your attorney will draw it up and take it to the judge."

"Anything else?"

"Yeah. You'll keep me involved with what's going on with him on a regular basis. I want that in writing, too. And you're not to tell him rotten things any more. Like I'd rather play golf than be with my son. I'll let you know if there's anything else."

Joan got up and walked over to the front window. She stood there for a few moments before she spoke again. "I'd be curious to find out if you could really prove that I was a part of it."

"Joan, your little pal Bruce almost shit his pants when my attorney confronted him. Imagine what she'd do to him in a courtroom. By the way," Kevin said, "he was quite taken with that perfume you've been wearing for years. What is it? Shalimar? Kinda funny, Joan. Every time I smell it, I think of you, too."

She turned and looked at him but didn't say anything.

"You should be going to jail, Joan, but you probably won't even lose your real estate license. Joey needs his mother," Kevin said. "Take the deal."

Joan nodded before turning back to the window.

Pulling away from the house, Kevin felt no sense of victory. Only relief. He was exhausted, but he knew he needed to talk to Sara before he went home. And it was much, much too complicated to explain over his car phone.

Sara reacted to his appearance almost the same way that Joan had. "Oh my God, Kevin!" she exclaimed when she opened the door. "What happened?"

"Sorry it's so late," he said, "but I really need to talk to my attorney."

The fireplace was crackling. Sara led him to a chair next to it and kept her hand on his arm as he sat down. It felt good. She was wearing jeans and a tight-fitting white pullover. *Very* tight-fitting, he noticed. "Wine, or stronger?" she asked.

"Wine," Kevin said. "Red, if you have it; what the hell, I've already got a headache."

Sara went into the kitchen and returned with a full glass for each of them. She pulled up an ottoman and sat down facing him. "C'mon, let's hear it."

Kevin told her everything in a monologue. The hit-and-run, seeing Willie at the hospital, the red paint on the Mercedes, the 911 call, the confrontation on the 18th tee, Jack's death, and the meeting with Joan. It took him a half-hour and a second glass of wine. When he was finished, he shrugged his shoulders.

"Jesus," Sara said. "Hell of a night, huh?"

Kevin's eyebrows went up and he nodded. He held out his empty glass.

"Few questions first," she said. "Did you identify yourself when you called Nine-One-One?"

"No."

"And you didn't tell the police about Leonard's death?"

"That was the last thing I wanted to do."

"You have to, Kevin," Sara said. "And you have to do it now."

"Sara…"

She put a hand on his arm. "Listen to me. I know this has been a nightmare, but we have to tell the police what happened. What if someone saw you going out to the tee, or coming back? They find the body, they ask around, and someone tells them that you go out there every night. Guess who they're gonna want to talk to? They'll determine time of death, Kevin. So unless you lie, and I wouldn't advise you to do that, they'll know you were there at the same time. You said he broke through a fence when he attacked you, right?"

"Yes."

"A 'jumper' wouldn't do that, Kevin. It's a sign of a struggle. And that takes more than one person. Trust me," Sara said. "We have to go to them before they come to us."

"Shit," Kevin said.

On the way to the police station, Kevin asked Sara if he was going to get in trouble for not making a report earlier. "They won't like it, that's for sure," Sara answered, "and it'll make them a little suspicious, but it's not unheard-of behavior, either. What happened had to have been quite a shock. A frightening experience for anyone. But with you being an employee of Pebble Beach, and with the tournament still going on, and being in the playoff tomorrow, it's understandable that you might not be thinking clearly and report it right away. When the shock and confusion wore off, you went to your attorney and now we're reporting it."

"What about Joan?"

"As your attorney," Sara said, "I think you should tell them about her and protect yourself. Now and in the future. She tried to hurt you, Kevin."

"I know." He looked out the passenger-side window and thought of Joey.

"Whatever you decide," Sara said.

The interview was conducted by a burly detective named Mizner. He was a golfer and had been following the Pro-Am in the newspaper. He was polite the whole time, asked a lot of questions, and said, "Sure, uh-huh," a lot. When Kevin had finished telling him everything, Mizner had him write it all down in longhand. He then had Kevin sign the statement. Shortly before midnight, the detective told Kevin he could go and wished him luck in the playoff. He also said he'd be "in touch."

Kevin called the Tour's Director of Communications from Sara's place and told him about the night's events. "Un-fuck-ing-believable," Gardner said. "What the hell next, Kevin?"

"What else *could* happen, Richard?"

While he talked, Sara handed him a glass of red wine and lingered to look into his eyes. It made him forget what he was hearing for a moment. "What was that, Richard? Hang on." He asked Sara if she had a fax machine in her home office; Gardner wanted a copy of the police report. She nodded. "Yeah, there's one here, Richard. What's the number?" Kevin wrote it down. "Got it. Yeah, okay. No. Forget it, I'm not meeting with the media before the playoff. What? I don't know, it depends on when the police want to talk to me again." He took a sip of wine. Sara was still looking at him, smiling now. She looked...*frisky*, Kevin decided. "Say again, Richard? Look, I understand your position but I've got enough to deal with as it is. Yeah, all right. I'll see you in the morning."

Kevin hung up the phone and took the police report into Sara's office. When he'd finished faxing it, he came back into the kitchen, set the paper on the counter, sighed heavily, smiled, then took another sip of his wine.

Sara came over and stood in front of him again. "You need to go to bed," she said.

"Yeah, I know, but I think I'm too wound up to sleep. What I really need," he said, "is a long, hot shower."

Sara smiled and moved closer to him. *Real* close. "As your attorney," she said, "I'm advising you that that is a *wonderful* idea."

You were right, Richard, Kevin thought. *What the hell next?*

CHAPTER 16

He awoke at 5:00 a.m. after maybe three hours of sleep. For a moment, Kevin didn't know where he was. But then Sara stirred, and the previous night's events all came rushing back at him. *Jesus*, he thought.

He slipped carefully out of bed and went into the bathroom and peed. In the kitchen, he found the stuff he needed and made a pot of coffee. While it was brewing, he took another hot shower and used one of Sara's disposable razors to shave. He was also happy to find several new toothbrushes in her cabinet, and a bottle of aspirin. He swallowed four of the tablets.

At 6:00 a.m., Kevin called the pro shop and told Jerry that he needed some clothes for the playoff. His assistant didn't ask why and Kevin didn't explain it. Jerry simply asked for the size of each item, and where to make the delivery. Kevin told him. "Twenty minutes," Jerry said.

Kevin next called the switchboard at The Lodge and asked to be put through to Gil Maxwell's room. When the Tour official answered, Kevin told him who it was. "You hear about last night, Gil?"

"Oh, yeah," Maxwell replied. "Early this morning. You should've stayed on the Tour, Kevin. A lot safer than those club jobs."

"No shit."

"I take it you're still going to play."

"Definitely," Kevin said.

"Okay. Well, obviously we'll be beefing up security. I don't know for sure yet, but I assume there'll be some police in the crowd, too. It's going to be one of those 'media events,' Kevin," Maxwell said. "You ready for that?"

"No, but I don't see that I have any choice."

"You could always pull out, you know."

"Can't," Kevin said. "Too much at stake."

"Attaboy," Maxwell said. "I'll see you on 15 tee at 9:00 o'clock."

As Jerry had promised, he delivered the clothes before 6:30. Kevin was fully dressed when he went in to wake up Sara. She smiled dreamily after she opened her eyes. "And where do you think *you're* going?"

"I'm afraid I have to go to work."

"Have to?"

"Yup."

Sara faked a frown, then smiled again. "I need a half an hour."

"Good," Kevin said, "'cause that's all you got."

She sat up, hugged him, then climbed out of bed and walked into the bathroom.

Gil Maxwell's suggestion that the playoff was going to be a media event was hardly accurate. Zoo was more like it. Spectators, photographers, reporters, officials, marshals, security people and TV cameras were everywhere when they arrived at the course. Kevin held Sara's hand tightly as they were escorted through the crowd and into the pro shop. Jerry immediately handed Kevin a small piece of pink paper with a telephone message on it:

Sorry the team didn't make the cut, pro.
You'll have to save Pebble Beach all by
yourself. Kick ass.
Larry Caldwell

The note made Kevin smile. It also—for some reason—relaxed him. He looked at Sara. "You sure you want to go out there and watch?"

"Hell, yeah," she said. "I love football crowds."

"Jerry, can you go around with her?"

"You're the boss," he said. "Whatever you want me to do. Better get going, Kevin. Your clubs and the courtesy car are out back." He shook Kevin's hand. "Fairways and greens," he said.

Kevin turned to Sara again. "Have fun."

"You, too," she said. She raised up and gave him a light kiss on the lips. "Don't forget now. When you're thanking everybody on national TV, it's Sara *Arnold*."

Kevin smiled. "I'll try to remember."

Johnny Osborne was waiting when Kevin arrived at the practice range. He pulled the golf bag out of the trunk as soon as the driver popped it open.

"Thanks for helping me out, Johnny," Kevin said. "I really appreciate it."

"Thanks for *asking*, Mr. Courtney," the teenager replied. "This is gonna be great."

"I hope you're right," Kevin said.

The crowd around the practice area was as thick and keyed-up as the one back at the pro shop. If any of them were aware of what had happened the night before, they weren't showing it. They were definitely in a party mood.

CBS Television, in an unprecedented move, was preempting its regular programming to cover the playoff. A cameraman followed Kevin and Johnny through the ropes and onto the practice tee and then positioned himself 30 feet away.

Clouds so low that Kevin felt he could almost touch them shrouded the tops of the firs and cypress trees at the end of the range. The dankness coated his navy wind shirt with minute particles of moisture, and it sent a chill through him. He was grateful that Jerry had brought a turtleneck to wear underneath instead of the golf shirt he had asked for. It would be even colder out by the water.

As he did his stretching exercises, he told himself to do his best to forget the gallery and television and Jack Leonard and Willie and Komoto and the bet. Kaori Noro was at the other end of the range. Kevin tried to ignore him, too.

During his first few practice swings with his wedge, Kevin focused on how his right thumb felt. Before they had left for the course, Sara made him a new bandage out of gauze and medical tape. Another swing with the wedge confirmed to him that she had done a beautiful job. The dressing felt tight and protective.

As he hit shots with each of his clubs, Kevin pictured Willie's finger moving slowly back and forth. By the time he got to his titanium driver, he felt that his tempo was excellent. He finished his session with a few 1-irons, the club he would probably use on the 15th tee, and followed it with four or five shots with his 7-iron, the club he expected to use on his approach to the green. Hopefully, no more than that.

The same courtesy car driver took Kevin and Johnny back

to the putting green. Because he was antsy, Kevin spent as much time practicing his breathing as he did his stroke. He thought of the Lamaze classes that he and Joan had taken before Joey was born, and it helped.

Suddenly, it was time.

A marshal took them out to the 15th tee in a golf cart. Noro was already there. Neither player had acknowledged the other's presence on the practice tee, and there was no politeness here, either. Noro glanced at Kevin once, then looked away. To Kevin, it appeared as if the Japanese player was bored—as if Noro felt his opponent had rudely changed his travel plans and merely delayed the inevitable: he was going to win it anyway.

The two of them met Gil Maxwell in the middle of the tee. He was holding a golf cap upside down. "Pick a number, Kaori, and we'll see who hits first."

The day before, Noro's outfit had been red and white. Today, he was dressed entirely in black. *Who's death are you mourning?* Kevin thought. *Jack's or mine?*

The Japanese player took a small piece of paper from the cap and unfolded it. There was a 1 on it.

"You have the tee, Kaori," Maxwell said. "Play away. And good luck to both of you."

A murmur arose from the crowd as the two players went back to their bags—like two boxers going to their corners to await the bell. The noise quickly died, though, and there was silence by the time Noro was ready to hit. The hole they were about to play was a 398-yard, dogleg-left par 4. To the right off the tee—on the other side of a fence—was 17-Mile Drive. To the left, there were trees, bushes, and heavy rough.

Kaori went with his 3-wood and hit it long, to the right

center of the fairway and in perfect position to get at the back-left pin placement.

Kevin thought of Willie's metronome and took two smooth practice swings before drawing his 1-iron perfectly around the dogleg. His ball rolled to a stop 15 yards behind Noro's.

After he'd paced off the distance for Kevin's second shot, Johnny said, "45 to the front of the green, 67 to the flag." It was caddie shorthand for 145 yards and 167 yards.

Kevin nodded in agreement. The air was heavy but there didn't seem to be much wind in the way because of the trees. He pulled out his 7-iron and hit what he thought was a perfect shot—dead on line with the flagstick. An initial cheer from the spectators quickly turned to a groan when the ball landed on the front of the green, well short of the cup. Kevin closed his eyes in disappointment and wondered whether Willie would have detected the actual strength of the wind.

"Sorry, Mr. Courtney," Johnny said. "More wind than I thought, I guess."

"My fault, son, not yours."

Noro's 9-iron approach stopped within 15 feet of the cup. Kevin's putt was twice as long, but it was uphill and much straighter than his opponent's right-to-left slider. He looked at it, gave it a good stroke, but missed it to the right. He then breathed a sigh of relief when Kaori's ball broke left at the last second and stayed out.

"We dodged one there," Kevin whispered to Johnny as they were escorted through the crowd to the next hole. "Let's end this thing, huh?"

The caddie smiled broadly. "Okay by me, Mr. Courtney."

Kevin felt an increase in the wind off the water the moment he arrived at the tee. He looked up at the fast moving clouds and knew instantly that a storm was coming. It wasn't a question of *if* it would rain, but *when*. And whether his nerves could handle another delay.

Noro's tee-shot on the 402-yard, right-turning 16th was straight but not big; Kevin outdrove him by 20 yards. After watching Noro play a safe second to the center of the green, Kevin weighed the risks of going for the flag. The cup was cut in about the same spot it had been the day before, to the left and near the back of the green. On Sunday, Kevin's aggressive play had paid off with a birdie. But he'd been down by a shot and had been forced to gamble. That wasn't the case now. Having played safely, Noro would probably make par. Kevin stood in the fairway and wondered whether he should go for the three and risk making a five.

The rapidly darkening sky made his decision for him. His solidly hit 9-iron—almost a clone of the one he'd hit the day before—landed near Noro's ball, kicked to the left and rolled to within eight feet of the hole. In spite of the roar of approval that came from the spectators lining the hole, Kevin heard Johnny shout, "Awesome!"

Walking up to the green, Kevin had to fight hard to keep his emotions in check. Just like the putt he'd had on Sunday, he knew exactly what this one would do. He'd had it before, and he'd made it.

To no one's surprise, Kaori refused to let the impending storm make him hurry his putt. Slowly and carefully, he looked at the line from all four sides. Twice he conferred with his caddie, and twice he had the young man crouch behind the ball. Finally, he settled in over the putt—only to quickly back off and look at it once again.

Kevin's face remained passive. He was wondering whether

Noro really needed all these looks, or whether he just wanted Kevin to wait. The more time you gave your opponent time to think, the better the chances were that a negative thought would creep in. *Whatever*, Kevin thought. *I'm making it.*

Several spectators cheered loudly when Noro's birdie effort missed on the low side. His tap-in was followed by shouts of encouragement to Kevin. He heard the first few, then blocked out the rest. He studied the line, made two smooth practice strokes, thought of Willie's metronome, addressed the ball, looked once at the cup, took the blade back, then moved it forward. The gleaming white Titleist began to track perfectly. In seconds, it would break left into the right edge of the hole. Unconsciously, and uncharacteristically, Kevin started to raise both arms in a sign of final triumph. It was never completed. The ball caught the edge of the opening, appeared to start down, but instead made a circle and came to rest on the edge of the rim.

A mixture of sounds came from the huge gallery. Some groaned in disappointment, others seemed giddy and excited that the playoff would continue. Kevin stood staring at the ball for a moment, his face blank, then walked over and tapped it in. He handed Johnny his putter and the two of them followed the marshals to the next tee.

Not wanting to do it but unable to stop, Kevin found himself fighting the "ifs" as he walked. *If* the ball had gone in. *If* he had hit it a hair easier. *If* he hadn't played it quite so high. If the green hadn't been so wet. *If* Willie were here to advise him. *If, if.* He took a deep breath, let it out, and pulled on his glove. *Positives, Kevin. Only positives.*

The 17th at Pebble is a 209-yard par 3. Kevin knew that it was the hole where Nicklaus and Watson had won famous tournaments, and he wondered if it was where he would win one, too. A strange feeling came over him as he studied the wind-whipped flagstick in the distance. His anguish over the missed birdie had quickly turned to bitterness, then anger. It was a controlled anger, though, working in his favor. For some odd reason, he felt both calm and confident.

In keeping with the universal code that no true golfer ever reacts joyfully at his opponent's misfortune, Kevin showed no emotion when Noro's seemingly perfect 2-iron flew the green. From the tee, the ball actually appeared to have bounced over the cliff onto the beach below. The inexplicable shot, combined with Johnny's excited eyes and scattered shouts from the spectators, forced Kevin to focus even harder. Noro's ball could still be in play, and in a good lie. No matter where it was, the best player in the world could still make par. Kevin could not expect any help from the gods of golf; he had to do it himself.

The moment he hit his tee-shot, Kevin was sure it was the best 2-iron he'd ever hit in competition. What confirmed this feeling was the enormous roar that came from the crowd up ahead. The ball had stopped five feet from the flag.

The chant began even before they reached the green. *Kev-in, Kev-in, Kev-in!* It was as if he were one of the most beloved players in golf—a Freddie Couples-type player—someone admired for both his ability and his humbleness. Kevin felt overwhelmed by the gallery's affection, but he knew he still had to concentrate. It wasn't over yet. He tipped his cap, marked his ball, then gestured for quiet.

Noro's ball was in a rocky area, some eight feet below the cliff. Kevin and Johnny stood off to the side of the green and waited. Twice, the Japanese star came up the hill to check the flagstick's location. Twice, as well, he backed off the shot. Ready finally, he clipped the ball cleanly and pitched onto the putting surface. When it stopped rolling, it was six inches from the cup.

The amazing recovery for par clearly rattled Kevin. As much as he'd tried hard to *expect* his opponent to pull off a shot like that, he really didn't think he could do it. When he did, he took Kevin's confidence with him. Thinking defensively now, knowing he couldn't charge it and risk three-putting, Kevin left his birdie attempt short of the hole. The weak effort caused the gallery to groan loudly, and it made him feel like a coward. He felt himself blushing.

It started to rain as they walked to the 18th tee and quickly grew in intensity. Johnny took out the umbrella, popped it open and handed it to his player. Kevin held it over their heads as they waited for Noro to tee-off. Childishly, Kevin felt he didn't deserve to be dry. To so badly miss a putt that close to the cup—a putt that important—was something unforgivable to anyone who played professional golf.

Waiting for Noro, Kevin turned around and looked at the broken fence at the back of the tee. Yellow police tape was stretched across the opening. It made him think of something Jack Leonard had said the night before:

I didn't think you had a chance.

The sound of Kaori's tee-shot caused Kevin to turn around again. As he and everyone else expected, the ball came down in perfect position on the right side of the fairway. Only the soft, wet ground prevented it from being an exceptionally long drive. Off to the west, somewhere out over the water, there was thunder.

Accepting his driver from Johnny, Kevin teed up his ball

and began his preshot routine. Even though he and Noro were tied, he had the sense that he was behind in the play-off. It was not a good feeling but he couldn't shake it. All he could do was swing.

At first, the ball seemed to be traveling on the same line as Noro's. But then the wind caught it, and it drifted to the right, and it finally came down somewhere close to the big tree on the right of the fairway. Because of the pelting rain, it was hard to tell from the tee exactly where the ball had come to rest. Maybe—just like he had on Friday—Kevin had gotten lucky, and the ball was clear. Only Kevin knew for sure; he *knew* he didn't have a shot.

If the ball had stopped three feet shorter or three feet further, he could have at least used a mid-iron and punched the ball a hundred yards up the fairway. He looked to his right again, then to his left, and finally decided that he simply could not take a chance on hitting the tree. He took out his 7-iron, choked down on the shaft, and bumped the ball several yards ahead. It was all he could do.

Walking up to where Johnny was now standing, Kevin gave himself a pep talk. *This is no time to quit now, Kevin. You've worked too hard and come too far. Anything can happen, just like it did for Noro on the last hole. Keep grinding.*

He was still away, well over 200 yards from the green. Like the day before, the smart shot was a layup with a 5-iron in order to leave him with a wedge into the pin. A par was not out of the question. He pulled the club, dried the grip, and began his preshot routine. The grip continued to feel slick. He handed the club to Johnny and watched him work on it. Accepting it again, feeling it slip once more, Kevin suddenly realized that his wet glove was the problem.

"Johnny, see if there's another glove in my bag somewhere," Kevin said. He yanked at the Velcro strap and pulled off the wet glove. He looked over at Noro and could tell by his body language that he was annoyed by the delay. *Screw you,* Kevin thought. It was much too important a shot to take a chance on the club slipping. Even *no glove* would be better than a wet one.

When Johnny said, "This is the only one I could find," Kevin looked at him.

His caddie was holding a piece of white cloth in one hand and a white glove in the other. It was the glove that Willie had given him, Tom Watson's glove.

Kevin took it, pulled it on and tightened it. He made a fist. The glove was soft, dry, and a perfect fit. He looked up ahead through the rain at the green, then back at his caddie. Johnny was drying the grip on the 5-iron.

"Hang on a second, son," Kevin said. "How far we got to the hole?"

Johnny looked at him for a moment, a puzzled expression on his face, then broke into a broad grin. He put the club back, laid down the bag, and pulled out his yardage book. Two times he looked at landmarks to determine their distance on the pages. It took the teenager maybe a minute. Finally satisfied with his calculations, he said, "Two-ten to carry the bunker, two-forty-three to the flag. One-club wind. Against." He lifted the bag and stood it up. Smiling again, he said, "You got this shot."

Kevin took the headcover off his driver, pulled it out and dried the grip. It felt sticky. Settling in over the ball finally, he swung the club back beyond horizontal before reversing its direction and exploding it into the Titleist 3. Halfway to its

212

target, the ball disappeared in the gloom. For nearly 10 seconds, Kevin heard only the noise of the rain pelting his umbrella and a single sentence that came from his caddie. "Go, baby, go!" Johnny cried.

But then another sound came rolling back from the distant green. It was a roar that came from the crowd up ahead, an eruption that could only mean one thing: Kevin's ball was somewhere on the putting surface.

The miraculous shot—wherever it was; no one near Kevin could see that far through the rain—caused Noro to change his game plan. Instead of laying up and relying on his superb short game to make birdie, as his caddie clearly wanted him to do, the Japanese star decided to go for the green with his 3-wood. The moment the ball left the metal clubface, Kevin could tell by the sound that he'd struck it solidly. He stood next to Johnny and waited for a reaction from the crowd.

When it came, momentarily, the roar was even louder than the first one. Kevin's chin dropped and his heart sank, and he and Johnny began walking to the green. Noro, though, and his caddie, and hundreds of spectators, began running, racing up the fairway to see where the two balls lay. *He's closer,* Kevin thought. *That's what champions do.* The cheering up ahead continued.

Only when they were within 100 yards of the green did Kevin and his caddie see what had happened. Noro was standing in the front bunker, his second shot plugged high up into the face of the wet sand. Next to the flagstick, less than a foot away, was Kevin's ball.

Just like Kevin's third shot, Noro's third was equally miraculous. Kevin couldn't imagine anyone other than the best player in the world getting the ball from such an ugly lie to within 20 feet of the cup, as Noro did. His putt for birdie, though—possibly because he felt the gods of golf were pulling for someone else—never had a chance. Noro tapped in for his par, then acknowledged the applause from the spectators with a tip of his cap and a slight bow.

Days later, Kevin would not remember making the putt for the win. He would remember lining it up, remember standing over the ball, remember the roar from the crowd, remember Noro shaking his hand and telling him "Great shot," and remember the hugs from Johnny and Sara. But the stroke itself, and the ball falling into the cup, somehow got jettisoned to the far reaches of his mind. Kevin didn't care.

In between going to the Media Center and going to the hospital to visit Willie, he used Sara's cell phone to make a call.

"Hey, Joey, guess what?"

"Can't guess, Dad."

"I won it," Kevin said happily. "Son, I won it all."